Glimmers of Distant Stars

Emmanuel Dumbuya

Published by Emmanuel Dumbuya (ODUMZ), 2025.

This is a work of fiction. Similarities to real people, places, or events are entirely coincidental.

GLIMMERS OF DISTANT STARS

First edition. February 2, 2025.

Copyright © 2025 Emmanuel Dumbuya.

ISBN: 979-8230660378

Written by Emmanuel Dumbuya.

Also by Emmanuel Dumbuya

Africanah
Obelisk
Pandemic
The African Market
Kylian Mbappé
Glimmers of Distant Stars
Offline Souls: Escaping the Digital Noise

Watch for more at https://www.amazon.com/-/e/B0DPR9HGHJ.

Table of Contents

FOREWORD 1
CHAPTER ONE 3
CHAPTER TWO 5
CHAPTER THREE 9
CHAPTER FOUR 14
CHAPTER FIVE 19
CHAPTER SIX 24
CHAPTER SEVEN 29
CHAPTER EIGHT 35
CHAPTER NINE 40
CHAPTER TEN 45
CHAPTER ELEVEN 50
CHAPTER TWELVE 55
CHAPTER THIRTEEN 60
CHAPTER FOURTEEN 65
CHAPTER FIFTEEN 71
CHAPTER SIXTEEN 77
CHAPTER SEVENTEEN 83
CHAPTER EIGHTEEN 89
CHAPTER NINETEEN 95
CHAPTER TWENTY 101

To Prof. Bashiru Mohamed Koroma, Vice Chancellor and Principal, Njala University, Sierra Leone, West Africa. Your visionary leadership and unwavering commitment to education and innovation have been a guiding light in my journey. This work is dedicated to you, for your tireless dedication to shaping minds, empowering communities, and fostering a future of boundless possibilities for Africa. Your influence continues to inspire and illuminate the path forward for us all.

With deepest gratitude,

"The stars above are not just lights in the sky; they are reflections of our dreams, our potential, and the future we are destined to shape."— **Emmanuel Dumbuya**

FOREWORD

In the vast expanse of the cosmos, stars have long served as symbols of aspiration, their steady light guiding civilizations toward progress and enlightenment. *Glimmers of Distant Stars* embarks on an extraordinary journey to reimagine Africa's place in the universe—not as a continent weighed down by challenges, but as a vibrant beacon of innovation, resilience, and boundless potential. Through the lens of speculative fiction, this narrative envisions a future where African nations stand at the forefront of technology and innovation, redefining their place on the global stage and challenging entrenched stereotypes. It offers not just a vision of hope, but a tangible blueprint for a continent ready to lead with purpose and pride.

This work is a celebration of the transformative power of imagination. It demonstrates how stories can break free from conventional boundaries, offering new perspectives that reshape realities. As you journey through these pages, you are invited to witness the fusion of tradition and technology—a harmonious blending of Africa's rich cultural heritage with the cutting-edge innovations that will propel societies into a future defined by sustainable development, social equity, and cultural renaissance.

In this world, Africa is not merely catching up; it is carving a path toward a brighter tomorrow, one where technology serves as a catalyst for change, and its people—grounded in ancient wisdom and empowered by modern tools—lead the charge. The stars that shimmer in the sky are no longer distant; they are reflected in the collective potential of Africa's people, their aspirations lighting the way forward.

As you turn these pages, may you not only discover a vision of Africa's boundless future, but also find inspiration in the realization that within each of us lies a spark—a star waiting to illuminate the path forward. May *Glimmers of Distant Stars* remind you that the future is ours to shape, and in the brilliance of our imagination, we hold the power to guide the world toward a new dawn.

CHAPTER ONE
THE DAWN OF TOMORROW

In the heart of Africa, a new day is breaking—a day where technology and tradition no longer exist in separate spheres, but instead coexist and collaborate to shape a vibrant and sustainable future. This is not just a vision of hope, but a reality in the making. As we stand on the threshold of this new era, Africa is embracing a future where its rich cultural heritage becomes the foundation for groundbreaking innovations that will resonate far beyond the continent's borders.

A Future Born from the Past

Africa's future is intricately tied to its past. The wisdom of ancient civilizations and the deeply rooted traditions that have sustained communities for centuries are being drawn upon to guide the continent into the technological age. Far from being a barrier, tradition is being woven into the fabric of modernity, creating a unique blueprint for innovation that is both forward-thinking and deeply connected to the land and its people.

This chapter sets the stage for a journey through the evolving landscape of African technological transformation. We will explore how this transformation is not merely about the adoption of the latest gadgets or systems, but about the reimagining of what it means to innovate in a way that respects and celebrates the continent's vast cultural diversity. From the rhythms of traditional drum circles to the algorithms of artificial intelligence, Africa is crafting a future where its past is not discarded but reinterpreted and revitalized for the challenges and opportunities of the 21st century.

Africa's Technological Renaissance

As the world grapples with unprecedented challenges—climate change, social inequality, and political instability—Africa stands at the crossroads of a remarkable renaissance. What was once perceived as a continent lagging behind in technological progress is now rapidly emerging as a global leader in innovation. From mobile banking to renewable energy solutions, Africa is not merely catching up with the rest of the world; it is paving its own path, offering new models of technology that are uniquely African in both form and function.

But this leap forward is not just about technology for technology's sake. It is about leveraging technological advances to solve deeply entrenched problems—healthcare access, poverty, education, and infrastructure—while ensuring that these solutions are embedded in the values and traditions that have long shaped African societies.

Connecting the Global with the Local

In this new world, the global is intricately connected with the local. Africa's future is no longer defined solely by external forces but by its own hands and hearts. The digital revolution is being met with local ingenuity, as African innovators take ownership of the technologies they develop. It is a world where mobile apps are designed not just for convenience but to address the real, pressing needs of local communities—from agricultural tools that help farmers optimize their crops to healthcare platforms that provide remote medical consultations in rural areas.

In this vision of tomorrow, the digital divide is not an insurmountable chasm, but a bridge that is being built by young African entrepreneurs, scientists, and artists, who are using the tools of the digital age to advance their own narratives and tell their own stories. Africa's future will not be dictated by foreign powers, but will be driven by Africans themselves, rooted in local realities but reaching for global aspirations.

As we embark on this journey through "The Dawn of Tomorrow," we are witnessing the birth of a new era—one where technology and tradition are not opposites but partners in creating a future that is as much about preserving the past as it is about shaping what is to come.

CHAPTER TWO

ECHOES OF THE ANCESTORS

In the heart of Africa, the past is never truly gone. It lingers in the wind, the songs, the rituals, and the languages—a persistent echo that reverberates through generations. This chapter explores how ancient African wisdom, passed down through storytelling, communal practices, and oral traditions, is not a relic of the past but a living, breathing force that shapes the present and future. In a rapidly changing world, these ancestral teachings are not only being preserved, but they are also providing the foundation for some of the most innovative advancements of the 21st century.

The Wisdom of the Ancestors: A Timeless Compass

For millennia, African societies have thrived by adhering to principles of balance, respect for nature, community, and sustainability. These values were embedded in every aspect of life—from the methods of agriculture that harmonized with the land, to the spiritual beliefs that connected the physical and spiritual worlds. The wisdom of the ancestors was a guide to living well in both the material and immaterial realms, offering insights into the human experience that continue to be relevant today.

In the modern context, these principles are being reinterpreted and integrated into the innovative practices that are reshaping Africa's future. For example, traditional ecological knowledge—passed down from generation to generation—is now being combined with modern environmental science to create sustainable farming practices and climate-resilient crops. Farmers who have lived on the land for centuries understand the rhythms of nature, and they are now applying this knowledge alongside new technologies to improve food security across the continent.

Innovation Rooted in Tradition

While many view innovation as a product of modernity, in Africa, it is often deeply rooted in tradition. The concept of "ubuntu," a Nguni Bantu term that means "I am because we are," is a guiding principle for many African communities. It emphasizes interconnectedness, mutual respect, and collective well-being. This philosophy is now being applied to modern social enterprises, where businesses are not solely focused on profit but on uplifting entire communities. Technology solutions are being developed with a deep understanding of the social fabric, ensuring that innovation serves the collective good.

One of the most striking examples of this fusion is seen in the way African designers and entrepreneurs are blending traditional African aesthetics with cutting-edge technologies. Fashion designers are incorporating indigenous fabrics and patterns into smart clothing, while engineers are integrating African-inspired designs into sustainable infrastructure. This blending of the old and new is creating a uniquely African blueprint for the future, where tradition informs and enriches innovation.

Healing through Ancient Knowledge

Traditional African medicine, with its roots in herbal remedies and holistic healing, has long been a cornerstone of African life. Today, these ancient practices are being revitalized and integrated into modern healthcare systems. Researchers are now studying indigenous plants that have been used for centuries for their medicinal properties, hoping to uncover new treatments for contemporary diseases. In many cases, these plants hold the key to addressing health challenges that modern medicine has not yet been able to solve.

In addition, the communal approach to healthcare, where entire communities take responsibility for the well-being of each other, is being incorporated into modern health strategies. Mobile health platforms that facilitate access to medical consultations and information are designed not only with technology in mind, but with an understanding of the importance of community care, respect for elders, and the sharing of resources.

Bridging the Digital Divide: Ancestral Knowledge Meets Technology

In the realm of education, Africa's ancient systems of knowledge transmission—chiefly oral and experiential—are now being combined with the digital age. Universities and tech hubs across the continent are developing platforms that incorporate indigenous knowledge systems, offering students access to traditional ways of knowing while equipping them with modern skills in science, technology, engineering, and mathematics (STEM). These platforms celebrate the cultural richness of African languages and promote storytelling as a means of sharing knowledge, giving rise to a generation of young Africans who are both rooted in their heritage and empowered by the tools of the future.

The integration of technology with traditional knowledge is particularly evident in the preservation and revitalization of African languages. Apps are being developed to teach indigenous languages, ensuring that the wisdom embedded in these languages is passed on to future generations. This digital innovation is not just about preserving the past; it is about revitalizing and adapting cultural practices to suit the needs of contemporary society.

The Call of the Ancestors: A Sustainable Future

As Africa strides confidently into the future, it does so with a deep respect for its ancestors and their timeless wisdom. Ancient African principles are proving to be not only relevant but also essential in shaping solutions to modern challenges. The lessons learned from the past are the key to unlocking a future that is sustainable, equitable, and technologically advanced.

In this chapter, we have witnessed the intricate ways in which the echoes of the ancestors are guiding Africa's innovation journey. From agriculture to healthcare, from education to the arts, ancient wisdom is being interwoven with modern advancements, creating a powerful synergy that honors the past while embracing the future.

As we move forward, we must not forget the lessons of the past. The ancestors' whispers continue to guide us, reminding us that progress is not only about technological advancement but about preserving and nurturing the values that make us human. By looking back, we find the clarity to move forward. In the next chapter, we will explore the ways in which Africa's rich cultural heritage will continue to shape its future as it leads the world in innovation, sustainability, and unity.

CHAPTER THREE

THE SILICON SAVANNAH

The sun rises over the sprawling cityscape of Nairobi, casting its golden light on a landscape that, just a few decades ago, seemed far removed from the world of high-tech innovation. Today, it is the beating heart of Africa's digital renaissance—*The Silicon Savannah*. This is where Africa's future is being written, not in ink on paper, but in lines of code, in entrepreneurial zeal, and in the unyielding drive of a generation determined to reshape the continent's destiny.

The term "Silicon Savannah" is a nod to the original tech haven of Silicon Valley in the United States, but it is uniquely African. It represents more than just technology; it symbolizes a space where Africa's challenges and opportunities converge, where innovation and tradition coalesce, and where the spirit of entrepreneurship is not just encouraged but thrives. In this chapter, we will explore the flourishing tech ecosystem that is transforming Africa, positioning the continent as a global leader in technology, and reimagining what the future holds for its people.

A New Era of Innovation

As the world's digital economy expands, Africa is stepping up to claim its place on the global stage. The Silicon Savannah is not just a symbol; it is a real, palpable phenomenon. Cities like Nairobi, Lagos, Accra, and Cape Town are rapidly evolving into major tech hubs, attracting investors, entrepreneurs, and tech enthusiasts from across the world. The continent's young, dynamic population, with its unparalleled creativity and adaptability, is leading the charge. These cities are where the ideas of tomorrow are born, fueled by a new breed of innovators who are rethinking everything from mobile banking to renewable energy solutions.

In Nairobi, the vibrant tech ecosystem is built on a foundation of collaboration and inclusivity. Startups, incubators, and accelerators flourish here, all working toward a shared goal: creating scalable, sustainable solutions to Africa's most pressing challenges. From M-Pesa, the groundbreaking mobile money service, to the burgeoning digital health startups that are revolutionizing healthcare access, the Silicon Savannah is proof that the continent is no longer playing catch-up—it is driving change.

Tech as a Catalyst for Economic Transformation

In many African nations, technology is a powerful catalyst for economic growth and social change. With internet connectivity improving rapidly, even in remote rural areas, the digital divide is shrinking. Innovations in mobile technology are enabling farmers to access real-time market prices, empowering women entrepreneurs to expand their businesses, and giving young people the tools to engage in the global digital economy.

The rise of e-commerce platforms, fintech startups, and digital platforms for education has unleashed a wave of entrepreneurship across the continent. Young Africans are harnessing the power of technology to build solutions that cater to local needs, transforming industries such as agriculture, healthcare, education, and finance. With minimal initial investment, these tech-savvy innovators are solving problems in creative ways, bypassing the traditional barriers to business that have held back previous generations.

The Rise of a New Digital Economy

The Silicon Savannah is not only fostering innovation but also nurturing a new digital economy. Africa's tech revolution is reshaping industries and creating new jobs. From software development to data analytics, cybersecurity to digital marketing, the demand for skilled professionals is surging. Tech education is booming, with coding boot camps and online learning platforms empowering young Africans to build the skills needed to thrive in a digital world.

This new economy is also creating new pathways for cross-border collaboration and trade. Digital platforms are enabling African businesses to connect with international markets, breaking down geographical and infrastructural barriers. The continent's entrepreneurial spirit, coupled with the power of technology, is positioning Africa to be a key player in the global economy.

The Role of Government and Policy in Fostering Innovation

While the entrepreneurial spirit in the Silicon Savannah is palpable, it would not have flourished without the support of forward-thinking governments and policies. In many countries, governments are recognizing the transformative power of technology and are actively working to foster an environment conducive to innovation.

Through initiatives such as tax incentives for tech startups, investments in infrastructure and the creation of innovation hubs, African governments are laying the groundwork for a digital future. Furthermore, the commitment to improving digital literacy and internet access is helping bridge the gap between urban and rural populations, ensuring that the benefits of the digital economy are felt by all.

In Kenya, the government's support of the tech sector has resulted in the rise of *Silicon Savannah* as a beacon of African innovation. The Kenyan government has invested heavily in improving the country's digital infrastructure, which has laid the foundation for a thriving tech ecosystem. Policies that encourage entrepreneurship, coupled with access to venture capital, have given birth to some of Africa's most successful startups.

Challenges on the Path to the Future

While the success stories of the Silicon Savannah are inspiring, they do not come without challenges. Despite the rapid growth of the tech industry, Africa still faces obstacles such as inadequate infrastructure, lack of access to affordable internet, and the brain drain of young talent seeking opportunities abroad. Additionally, the need for comprehensive cybersecurity measures is increasing as digital transformation spreads across the continent.

However, these challenges are not insurmountable. By leveraging Africa's unique strengths—its youth, its cultural diversity, and its collective ingenuity—there is immense potential to overcome these hurdles. The key lies in maintaining a collaborative approach, where governments, the private sector, and civil society work together to create a thriving digital economy that benefits all.

A Vision for the Future: Tech as a Tool for Sustainable Development

The Silicon Savannah is not just about building the latest tech gadgets or becoming a global leader in digital innovation; it is about using technology as a tool to address the most pressing challenges Africa faces. Sustainable development, poverty eradication, and environmental conservation are at the heart of Africa's digital revolution. From solar-powered tech solutions to mobile applications that promote environmental conservation, the tech ecosystem is constantly evolving to address Africa's unique development needs.

In the years to come, the Silicon Savannah is poised to become the epicenter of Africa's sustainable development agenda. By aligning technological innovation with the continent's priorities—empowering local communities, promoting inclusive growth, and preserving the environment—Africa is setting the stage for a future where technology is used not only to drive economic growth but also to improve the quality of life for all its people.

As the world watches, the Silicon Savannah stands as a beacon of Africa's digital potential. It represents a future where technology and tradition do not exist in opposition, but in harmony. It is a future where the innovative spirit of Africa's youth, combined with the continent's deep cultural roots, creates solutions that are as unique as the land they come from. The Silicon Savannah is not just Africa's digital hub; it is the world's digital frontier.

CHAPTER FOUR

VOICES OF THE DIASPORA

Africa's global diaspora has always been a wellspring of talent, ingenuity, and resilience. From the bustling streets of London and New York to the innovative tech hubs of Berlin and Toronto, millions of Africans have sought opportunities abroad, often propelled by the promise of a better future. Yet, despite their physical distance, their hearts remain tethered to the continent they call home. This chapter explores the dynamic role African expatriates play in shaping the future of the continent's technological landscape, acting as bridges between Africa and the world, and contributing to its digital revolution from afar.

The Transnational Tech Revolution

The African diaspora has long been an integral part of Africa's development, both socially and economically. However, in recent years, this role has evolved. As technology continues to reshape the global landscape, the African diaspora has increasingly found itself in a unique position to influence the continent's technological progress. Many expatriates have become pivotal players in the world of Silicon Valley, Europe's fintech markets, and emerging tech hubs in Asia, all while maintaining deep ties to their countries of origin.

From the launch of mobile applications and digital platforms to the establishment of startups and partnerships, the African diaspora has helped transform the tech industry in Africa. They bring a wealth of knowledge, experience, and investment that is essential to the growth of the continent's digital economy. Through mentorship, investments in local startups, and the creation of transnational networks, the diaspora is helping build bridges that connect African innovators with global markets.

Diaspora-Driven Startups: Innovation across Borders

In cities like Lagos, Nairobi, and Cape Town, numerous startups have emerged, often with the guiding hands of those in the diaspora. These entrepreneurs, who have honed their skills abroad, return home or collaborate remotely to launch groundbreaking initiatives that address local challenges with global solutions.

One such example is *Andela*, a startup co-founded by African expatriates that trains software developers in Africa and connects them to global companies. What began as a small project has now grown into a global phenomenon, with Andela providing software development services from its offices in Nigeria, Kenya, and Uganda to clients in the United States and beyond. This is just one example of how the diaspora's influence has become a catalyst for change.

Diaspora-driven startups often target critical sectors such as fintech, e-commerce, health tech, and education, where they leverage the lessons learned abroad to create innovative solutions that are scalable across Africa. These ventures are not just about financial returns but also about improving livelihoods, increasing access to essential services, and fostering a culture of entrepreneurship that can transform entire communities.

Knowledge Transfer and Mentorship

In addition to launching businesses, African expatriates are playing an instrumental role in mentoring the next generation of innovators. Many diaspora professionals in the fields of tech, engineering, and business are dedicating time and resources to nurturing African talent. They offer mentorship, advisory services, and training programs that help bridge the skills gap between Africa and the more developed tech markets abroad.

Programs such as *Tech Mentors Africa* and *African Women in Tech* have emerged, providing mentorship opportunities for aspiring tech entrepreneurs. These initiatives not only offer professional guidance but also empower young African innovators, particularly women, to break into the tech industry. The diaspora's influence in these programs has proven invaluable, as it provides local tech enthusiasts with insights into the global tech landscape, equipping them with the skills necessary to succeed.

The diaspora's role in knowledge transfer is also seen in the rise of *coding boot camps* and online education platforms, many of which are founded by expatriates. These platforms offer affordable, high-quality tech training to young Africans, equipping them with the skills required to meet the demands of an increasingly digital world. By embracing digital education, these expatriates help build a future workforce that is globally competitive while ensuring that Africa's talent pool remains robust.

Investments: A Lifeline for Africa's Tech Ecosystem

For many years, Africa's access to venture capital and global investment has been limited. However, the African diaspora is increasingly stepping into the gap, making strategic investments that help scale local innovations and establish a sustainable tech ecosystem. Many diaspora investors have established venture funds specifically targeting African startups, providing seed capital and financial backing to promising tech ventures across the continent.

These investments are often directed toward solving local problems with scalable, sustainable solutions. For instance, fintech companies like *Paystack* and *Flutterwave* have secured significant investment from diasporan-led funds, which enabled them to grow rapidly and expand their reach across the continent. These companies are revolutionizing payment solutions, making it easier for businesses and individuals to engage in e-commerce and digital transactions.

Diaspora investors are also instrumental in supporting African-led ventures that focus on agriculture technology (AgriTech), renewable energy, and sustainable development—sectors that are key to Africa's long-term growth. Their financial contributions are helping to build the infrastructure necessary for the continent to thrive in the digital age.

The Role of African Diaspora Networks

The African diaspora is united not only by its shared heritage but also by its deep commitment to the advancement of the continent. Various diaspora networks and organizations are dedicated to fostering collaboration between African expatriates and local innovators. Networks like the *African Diaspora Network (ADN)* and *The African Diaspora Marketplace* provide platforms for diasporans to connect with African entrepreneurs, share ideas, and collaborate on projects that drive development.

These networks also serve as vital channels for raising awareness about Africa's growing tech ecosystem. By connecting African expatriates with investors, policymakers, and business leaders, they facilitate partnerships that promote the growth of Africa's digital economy. In the coming years, these networks will continue to be critical in fostering collaboration, sharing knowledge, and mobilizing resources for the benefit of Africa.

The Future of the Diaspora's Contribution

Looking forward, the role of the African diaspora in the continent's technological transformation is poised to expand. With the increasing digitization of Africa's economies and the global shift toward sustainable development, the diaspora's expertise and resources will be essential to driving innovation in areas such as renewable energy, digital health, and environmental sustainability.

The diaspora's impact will also be felt in the acceleration of Africa's digital transformation, particularly as more expatriates return to their home countries or continue to work remotely in partnership with local innovators. As digital infrastructure improves and more opportunities emerge, the contributions of the African diaspora will continue to play a pivotal role in shaping the future of the continent.

The voices of the diaspora are an integral part of Africa's story. They are not only contributing to the continent's technological advancements but are also ensuring that Africa's digital future is inclusive, sustainable, and transformative. As we continue to build bridges between the global African community and the continent, we will witness an even greater synergy between the diaspora and local innovators, one that will help shape a more prosperous and digitally empowered Africa for generations to come.

CHAPTER FIVE

THE GREEN REVOLUTION

Africa, the cradle of agriculture, is experiencing a transformation unlike any other in its history. With its fertile soils, vast landscapes, and rich biodiversity, the continent is a natural powerhouse in the global agricultural sector. However, traditional farming practices have often struggled to meet the demands of a growing population and a changing climate. In this chapter, we explore how innovations in sustainable agriculture are not only addressing these challenges but are also poised to revolutionize African economies, ecosystems, and the lives of millions.

Reimagining African Agriculture: A New Paradigm

The Green Revolution in Africa is not just a return to ancient agricultural practices; it is a reimagining of how farming can be conducted in harmony with nature while embracing modern technology. Innovations in sustainable agriculture are driven by the need to adapt to climate change, improve food security, and create economic opportunities in rural communities.

In the past, the term "Green Revolution" often referred to the widespread adoption of high-yielding varieties of crops, chemical fertilizers, and modern farming techniques. However, the new Green Revolution in Africa is characterized by an integrated approach that emphasizes ecological balance, soil health, and water conservation, all while improving productivity. This paradigm shift aims to make farming both sustainable and profitable, allowing African countries to feed their growing populations and contribute to global food security.

Smart Agriculture: Harnessing Technology for Sustainability

Technology has become a key driver in Africa's agricultural transformation. Smart agriculture, which combines traditional knowledge with cutting-edge technologies such as artificial intelligence

(AI), drones, Internet of Things (IoT) devices, and precision farming techniques, is revolutionizing how farmers grow crops, manage resources, and optimize yields.

For instance, AI-powered platforms help farmers predict weather patterns, optimize irrigation schedules, and manage pests and diseases more effectively. Through remote sensing and satellite imagery, farmers can monitor the health of their crops in real-time and make data-driven decisions that increase crop yields while minimizing the use of harmful chemicals. By integrating technology, smallholder farmers can become more resilient to climate change and enhance their productivity without further degrading the land.

In countries like Kenya, Nigeria, and South Africa, digital tools such as mobile apps, agri-tech platforms, and e-commerce solutions are empowering farmers by providing access to market information, financial services, and agricultural inputs. These tools enable farmers to improve their livelihoods, while creating new opportunities for agribusinesses and investors.

Agroecology: Reviving Traditional Practices for a Sustainable Future

Agroecology, a farming system that seeks to balance productivity with environmental sustainability, is gaining momentum across Africa. This approach emphasizes the importance of preserving biodiversity, improving soil fertility, and reducing reliance on synthetic fertilizers and pesticides. By integrating indigenous farming knowledge with modern sustainable practices, Agroecology provides a powerful solution to the challenges faced by African farmers.

In countries like Ethiopia, Zambia, and Uganda, farmers are rediscovering ancient agricultural techniques that have been proven to work in harmony with the environment. These practices include crop rotation, agroforestry (growing trees alongside crops), and the use of organic fertilizers. Agroecology helps to restore ecosystems, enhance water retention, and protect against soil erosion, all while maintaining high levels of crop productivity.

Moreover, Agroecology empowers local communities to take charge of their food systems, ensuring food sovereignty and resilience in the face of climate change. It also supports the preservation of cultural traditions and strengthens local economies, as farmers grow diverse crops suited to their unique environments.

Sustainable Livestock Farming: Rethinking Animal Husbandry

Sustainable livestock farming is another crucial aspect of the Green Revolution in Africa. With Africa's population set to double by 2050, the demand for animal products such as meat, milk, and eggs will increase significantly. However, conventional livestock farming often leads to overgrazing, land degradation, and loss of biodiversity. Sustainable approaches to animal husbandry are essential for ensuring that livestock farming can continue to contribute to Africa's food security without causing long-term harm to the environment.

Techniques such as rotational grazing, where livestock is moved from one pasture to another to allow for grass regeneration, and the integration of animals into crop systems to improve soil fertility, are becoming more widely adopted. In addition, advancements in veterinary care, breeding techniques, and nutrition are helping farmers raise healthier animals while reducing environmental impacts.

For instance, the introduction of drought-resistant breeds of cattle, goats, and sheep has helped farmers in arid and semi-arid regions to withstand the challenges posed by climate change. These innovations are improving food security, income generation, and the livelihoods of millions of African pastoralists.

Hydroponics and Vertical Farming: Growing Food in Cities

As urbanization accelerates across Africa, the demand for locally grown food in cities is rising. However, urban farming faces numerous challenges, including limited space, water scarcity, and poor soil quality. Innovations such as hydroponics and vertical farming are providing solutions to these problems, enabling food production in even the most densely populated areas.

Hydroponics, the practice of growing plants in a nutrient-rich water solution without soil, is rapidly gaining popularity in cities like Nairobi, Lagos, and Cairo. This technique allows for year-round production of vegetables and herbs, using significantly less water and space compared to traditional farming. Vertical farming, which involves stacking crops in vertically arranged layers, also maximizes space and reduces the carbon footprint of food production.

These innovations are not only helping to meet the food demands of urban populations but are also creating new economic opportunities for entrepreneurs, particularly women and youth, who are entering the agriculture sector in innovative ways.

Sustainable Energy and Agriculture: A Symbiotic Relationship

The integration of renewable energy with agriculture is another key aspect of the Green Revolution in Africa. Many farmers across the continent lack reliable access to electricity, which limits their ability to operate modern equipment, store food, and process agricultural products. The adoption of solar, wind, and bioenergy solutions is helping to address this issue, enabling farmers to improve productivity and reduce post-harvest losses.

For example, solar-powered irrigation systems are providing water for crops in areas that were previously underserved, while solar dryers are reducing the spoilage of fruits and vegetables. By harnessing renewable energy, farmers can improve the efficiency and sustainability of their operations, while also reducing their carbon footprint.

The Role of Policy and Investment in Sustainable Agriculture

For the Green Revolution to succeed, it requires strong government support, private sector investment, and international cooperation. Governments must prioritize policies that promote sustainable agricultural practices, provide incentives for green innovations, and create an enabling environment for agri-tech startups and farmers. This includes investing in infrastructure, such as roads, storage facilities, and irrigation systems, which are essential for enhancing agricultural productivity.

Private sector investment is equally critical. Venture capitalists, international development organizations, and local investors must support the growth of sustainable agriculture businesses, from seed companies and fertilizer producers to agri-tech firms and food processors. Public-private partnerships are essential to scaling up innovations and ensuring that they reach smallholder farmers who stand to benefit the most.

The Green Revolution in Africa is not a distant dream—it is already underway. Through innovations in sustainable agriculture, Africa has the potential to become a global leader in food production, environmental stewardship, and economic development. By combining ancient wisdom with modern technology, the continent is laying the foundation for a sustainable agricultural future that benefits not only Africans but the entire world. As Africa continues to embrace its agricultural potential, it will ensure food security for its people, protect its ecosystems, and empower future generations of farmers to thrive.

CHAPTER SIX

DIGITAL NOMADS

In the heart of Africa, a new generation of entrepreneurs is emerging—individuals who are harnessing the power of technology to create global businesses without ever leaving their local communities. These "digital nomads" are redefining the traditional notions of work, business, and success. They are living proof that with the right tools, a Wi-Fi connection, and determination, young Africans can thrive in a digital world that once seemed far removed from their daily lives. This chapter explores the transformative stories of these digital pioneers who are breaking boundaries, building global enterprises, and revolutionizing Africa's economic landscape.

A New Age of Entrepreneurship

Traditionally, entrepreneurship in Africa has been rooted in physical commerce, with businesses often relying on local trade, market stalls, and regional connections. However, the rise of the digital economy has unlocked a new frontier. Today, young Africans are no longer limited by geography. They are reaching international markets, connecting with clients and partners from every corner of the globe, and leveraging digital platforms to build successful businesses from their home communities.

This shift is particularly pronounced among the youth, who, armed with laptops and smartphones, are using technology to offer a wide range of services—from software development and digital marketing to e-commerce and freelance consulting. In cities and villages across Africa, digital nomads are proving that success does not require physical proximity to major economic centers. Instead, they are pioneering a new form of entrepreneurship that prioritizes creativity, innovation, and global connectivity.

The Rise of African Tech Hubs

Across Africa, thriving tech hubs have emerged as epicenters of innovation and digital entrepreneurship. Cities like Nairobi, Lagos, Cape Town, and Accra have become well-known for their dynamic tech ecosystems, attracting digital nomads who are eager to tap into these growing markets. These hubs are not just places where people work—they are communities where ideas are born, collaborations are formed, and digital enterprises are nurtured.

The success of these tech hubs can be attributed to several factors: access to affordable internet, the growing adoption of mobile technology, and a thriving culture of innovation. For instance, Nairobi's "Silicon Savannah" has become home to some of the most successful startups in Africa, offering opportunities for digital nomads to collaborate with like-minded individuals, scale their businesses, and access venture capital.

The rise of tech hubs is particularly significant for young Africans, as it fosters a sense of belonging and encourages networking, mentorship, and collaboration. Through these spaces, young entrepreneurs can access tools and resources that were once inaccessible, leveling the playing field and enabling them to compete on the global stage.

The Digital Nomad Lifestyle: Freedom and Flexibility

One of the most appealing aspects of being a digital nomad is the freedom it offers. Unlike traditional business owners, digital nomads are not tied to a specific location. They can operate their enterprises from anywhere—be it a bustling urban center, a quiet rural village, or even while traveling across the continent or abroad.

This lifestyle has become increasingly popular among young Africans, many of whom seek the flexibility to work from anywhere, manage their own time, and pursue projects that align with their passions. The rise of co-working spaces, the availability of online marketplaces, and the democratization of business tools have made it easier than ever to start and run a global enterprise while staying rooted in Africa.

For some, this freedom means running a tech company from a small village in Tanzania, while for others, it may involve offering freelance writing or graphic design services to clients in the United States or Europe. Regardless of the industry, the digital nomad lifestyle has empowered young Africans to take control of their careers and build enterprises that transcend borders.

Technology as a Bridge to Global Opportunities

The role of technology in enabling African digital nomads cannot be overstated. The internet, mobile phones, and cloud computing have become the backbone of many businesses, connecting digital nomads with clients, suppliers, and collaborators around the world.

For example, a web developer in Lagos can build websites for clients in New York without ever leaving Nigeria. Similarly, a fashion designer in Accra can use platforms like Etsy or Instagram to sell handmade goods to customers in London or Tokyo. Social media, e-commerce platforms, and online marketplaces have leveled the playing field, allowing digital nomads to access global markets and gain visibility on an international scale.

Furthermore, the rise of online learning platforms has enabled young Africans to acquire the skills needed to thrive in the digital economy. Whether it's mastering coding, digital marketing, graphic design, or entrepreneurship, African digital nomads are increasingly turning to the internet to develop their skills and gain the knowledge required to build successful businesses.

Overcoming Challenges: Connectivity, Infrastructure, and Capital

While the opportunities for African digital nomads are vast, the path to success is not without challenges. Access to reliable internet and electricity remains a significant hurdle in many parts of the continent. Although tech hubs and urban areas may enjoy fast and stable internet connections, rural areas often face connectivity issues that limit the ability of digital nomads to work effectively.

Additionally, many African entrepreneurs struggle to access funding and investment for their businesses. While venture capital and angel investors are slowly starting to recognize the potential of African tech startups, the landscape remains challenging for young entrepreneurs seeking to scale their businesses.

Despite these challenges, digital nomads in Africa are finding creative solutions. Many are relying on mobile phones, which have become a lifeline for digital entrepreneurs, enabling them to access the internet, manage their businesses, and communicate with clients even in remote areas. Furthermore, innovative financing models, such as crowd funding and peer-to-peer lending, are helping to bridge the funding gap for young entrepreneurs who may not have access to traditional bank loans or venture capital.

Success Stories: Digital Nomads Leading the Way

Across the continent, numerous success stories highlight the potential of African digital nomads. From freelance graphic designers and digital marketers to tech startup founders and online educators, African entrepreneurs are showing the world what is possible when innovation and opportunity meet.

One such success story is that of **Simbarashe, a digital entrepreneur from Zimbabwe**, who built an e-commerce platform connecting local artisans with buyers around the world. Through his platform, small-scale artisans in Zimbabwe are now able to sell their products to international customers, creating sustainable livelihoods for themselves while preserving traditional craftsmanship.

In **Kenya, Miriam**, a young software developer, founded a tech company that specializes in providing cloud-based solutions to African businesses. Through her company, Miriam has helped dozens of small and medium-sized enterprises (SMEs) access affordable digital tools that improve their efficiency and reach.

These stories are just a glimpse of the thriving digital nomad movement across Africa. As the continent continues to embrace digital transformation, it is clear that the future belongs to those who are willing to leverage technology to create global enterprises from their local communities.

The Future of Africa's Digital Nomads

The rise of digital nomads in Africa represents a shift toward a more decentralized, flexible, and innovative economy. As technology continues to evolve, so too will the opportunities for young Africans to create businesses that have a global impact.

With the right infrastructure, policies, and support systems in place, Africa has the potential to become a hub for digital entrepreneurs who are not just building businesses but are also reshaping the narrative of what it means to be successful in a globalized world.

CHAPTER SEVEN
THE QUANTUM LEAP

The world is on the brink of a technological revolution, one that is poised to transform industries, scientific research, and the global economy. This revolution is driven by quantum computing, a field that harnesses the principles of quantum mechanics to process information in ways that classical computers cannot. In this chapter, we explore the impact of quantum computing on African scientific research, how it is shaping the future of the continent, and the opportunities and challenges that come with this cutting-edge technology.

Understanding Quantum Computing: A Brief Overview

Quantum computing is a radically different approach to computation, based on the strange and fascinating laws of quantum mechanics. Unlike traditional computers, which process data in binary form (using bits that represent either 0 or 1), quantum computers use quantum bits or "qubits," which can exist in multiple states simultaneously due to a phenomenon known as superposition. This ability to process vast amounts of data at once enables quantum computers to solve complex problems much faster than classical computers.

In addition to superposition, quantum computers also exploit another principle called entanglement, where qubits become linked together, such that the state of one qubit directly influences the state of another, even across vast distances. These principles open up possibilities for quantum computing that were previously unimaginable, particularly in fields like cryptography, drug discovery, materials science, and artificial intelligence.

Africa's Emergence as a Quantum Frontier

While the field of quantum computing is still in its infancy, Africa is beginning to make strides in embracing this transformative technology. Several African nations are laying the groundwork for the future of quantum research by investing in education, infrastructure, and collaborations with international quantum computing initiatives. These efforts are designed to ensure that African scientists and researchers can participate in and benefit from the quantum revolution, rather than be left behind.

South Africa is one of the continent's leading players in the quantum space, with initiatives like the University of the Witwatersrand's Quantum Computing and Communication Lab and the South African Quantum Computing Initiative (SAQCI). These institutions are working to develop quantum technologies and provide training for the next generation of quantum scientists and engineers.

In **Kenya**, the **Kenya National Innovation Agency** has taken steps to incorporate quantum computing into the national innovation agenda, and there is growing interest from the private sector to leverage quantum technologies for solving challenges in industries such as telecommunications, finance, and agriculture.

Across the continent, **Nigeria** is emerging as a hub for quantum research, with universities and research institutes investing in quantum education programs and collaborating with global leaders in the field. The University of Lagos, for instance, has started to incorporate quantum mechanics into its physics curriculum, aiming to equip African students with the knowledge needed to become leaders in quantum technology.

Implications for African Scientific Research

Quantum computing holds immense promise for African scientific research, particularly in areas that are crucial for the continent's development. From healthcare and agriculture to energy and climate change, quantum technologies can offer solutions to some of Africa's most pressing challenges.

Healthcare: Accelerating Drug Discovery and Personalized Medicine

GLIMMERS OF DISTANT STARS

One of the most exciting applications of quantum computing is in the field of healthcare. The ability to model molecular interactions at the quantum level could revolutionize drug discovery and lead to the development of new treatments for diseases that disproportionately affect Africa, such as malaria, tuberculosis, and HIV/AIDS.

Quantum computers have the potential to simulate complex biological systems with unparalleled precision, enabling researchers to understand how diseases operate at the molecular level. This could lead to the design of more effective drugs, tailored to the specific needs of African populations. Additionally, quantum algorithms can assist in personalized medicine, helping to develop treatments that are optimized for individual genetic profiles, improving patient outcomes across the continent.

Agriculture: Solving Africa's Food Security Challenges

Agriculture is the backbone of many African economies, and quantum computing could play a pivotal role in addressing the continent's food security challenges. By analyzing complex data related to soil health, weather patterns, and crop diseases, quantum computing could help optimize farming practices, improve crop yields, and enhance food distribution networks.

For example, quantum algorithms could model agricultural ecosystems with a level of detail that classical computers cannot achieve, identifying the most effective ways to increase productivity while minimizing environmental impact. This is particularly important for Africa, where changing climate patterns are increasingly affecting farming communities.

Energy: Revolutionizing Renewable Energy Solutions

Energy is another critical area where quantum computing could have a profound impact. Many African nations are heavily dependent on non-renewable energy sources, and quantum technologies could help accelerate the transition to clean, renewable energy by optimizing the design of more efficient solar cells, wind turbines, and energy storage systems.

Quantum computing can also aid in the development of new materials with unique properties, such as superconductors that operate at higher temperatures, making energy transmission more efficient. By harnessing these advances, Africa could leapfrog into a new era of sustainable energy production and consumption, reducing its carbon footprint and ensuring a more reliable and equitable energy supply for its people.

Climate Change: Modeling and Mitigating Environmental Impacts

The African continent is disproportionately affected by climate change, facing droughts, floods, and extreme weather events that threaten livelihoods, food security, and infrastructure. Quantum computing's ability to simulate complex environmental systems could enable African scientists to better understand and predict climate patterns, helping to mitigate the impact of climate change and develop adaptive strategies for vulnerable communities.

Quantum models could improve the accuracy of weather forecasts, allowing for more timely and effective responses to climate-related disasters. In addition, quantum computing could be used to design new materials for sustainable construction and infrastructure, reducing the environmental impact of urbanization in Africa's rapidly growing cities.

Barriers to Success: Connectivity, Infrastructure, and Investment

While the potential of quantum computing in Africa is immense, there are several barriers that must be addressed to fully unlock its benefits. Chief among these are issues of infrastructure, investment, and access to expertise.

Access to reliable internet and electricity remains a challenge in many parts of Africa, particularly in rural areas. As quantum computing requires a stable and high-performance computing environment, significant investments in infrastructure are needed to support this field's growth across the continent.

Moreover, quantum research and development require substantial financial resources. While global partnerships and funding opportunities are emerging, African nations must prioritize quantum research and allocate resources for education, training, and collaboration to build a robust ecosystem of quantum researchers and practitioners.

Preparing Africa's Future Quantum Workforce

The success of Africa's quantum revolution will depend on the continent's ability to develop a skilled workforce. As quantum computing is an advanced field that requires a deep understanding of both physics and computer science, there is an urgent need to invest in education and training programs that will equip students with the skills necessary to excel in this domain.

Across Africa, universities are beginning to offer specialized programs in quantum computing, and partnerships with international quantum research centers are providing African students with the opportunity to gain hands-on experience. However, the continent must continue to expand its efforts to build a diverse and talented pool of quantum scientists, engineers, and technologists who can drive innovation and contribute to the global quantum ecosystem.

A Quantum Future for Africa

As Africa embraces the possibilities of quantum computing, the continent stands at the threshold of a new era of scientific discovery and technological advancement. By leveraging the power of quantum technologies, African researchers can address some of the continent's most pressing challenges and position Africa as a leader in the global knowledge economy.

The quantum leap is not just about technology—it is about transforming Africa's future, creating new opportunities for growth, and advancing the scientific frontiers that will shape the world for generations to come.

CHAPTER EIGHT

SOLAR WINDS

As the world faces the dual crises of climate change and dwindling fossil fuel resources, the search for sustainable, renewable energy solutions has become one of the most pressing challenges of the 21st century. Africa, with its vast and untapped natural resources, is positioned to become a global leader in renewable energy production, particularly through harnessing the power of the sun and wind. In this chapter, we explore how Africa can leverage these two renewable energy sources—solar and wind—to power its cities and industries, reduce its dependence on fossil fuels, and achieve sustainable economic growth.

The African Energy Landscape: A Call for Change

Africa is rich in renewable energy potential. The continent receives some of the highest levels of solar radiation in the world, particularly in the Sahara Desert and sub-Saharan regions. Likewise, many African nations have access to strong wind corridors, especially along the coasts of countries like South Africa, Egypt, and Kenya. Despite this abundance, a significant portion of the continent's population still lacks access to reliable electricity, and many African countries remain heavily reliant on fossil fuels for energy production.

In recent years, however, there has been a growing recognition of the need for a paradigm shift toward clean, renewable energy sources. This shift is not only motivated by environmental concerns but also by the economic opportunities that renewable energy presents, such as job creation, reduced energy costs, and greater energy security.

The Rise of Solar Power: Lighting Up the Future

Solar energy is one of the most promising sources of renewable power for Africa, and it is already transforming the continent's energy landscape. With solar panels becoming more affordable and efficient, many African countries are investing in large-scale solar farms to meet the growing demand for electricity. These solar farms can provide power to both urban centers and remote rural areas, where grid infrastructure is often lacking.

Solar Power in the Desert: The Case of the Sahara

One of the most ambitious projects in the African solar energy space is the **Desertec** initiative, which aims to harness the vast solar potential of the Sahara Desert to produce electricity that can be exported to Europe and the rest of Africa. The project envisions the construction of a massive network of solar power plants, connecting countries across North Africa and Europe. If successful, it could become a game-changer for Africa's energy sector, providing clean electricity to millions of people while also contributing to global climate goals.

In **Morocco**, the **Noor Ouarzazate Solar Complex**, one of the largest solar power plants in the world, is already operational. This project is a model for Africa's solar future, demonstrating how large-scale solar projects can deliver reliable, sustainable power. Similarly, countries like **Kenya** and **South Africa** are also investing in solar projects that integrate both grid and off-grid solutions to provide energy to urban and rural populations alike.

Solar for Rural Development: Off-Grid Solutions

While large-scale solar farms are crucial for meeting the continent's energy needs, off-grid solar solutions are equally important for reaching remote and underserved communities. Off-grid solar systems, which include solar home kits and solar-powered mini-grids, are providing affordable and sustainable electricity to millions of people in rural areas.

In **Kenya**, for example, the company **M-KOPA Solar** has pioneered the use of pay-as-you-go solar systems, enabling low-income households to purchase solar panels through affordable installment payments. This model has already transformed the lives of over one million people in East Africa, providing them with access to electricity for lighting, mobile phone charging, and small appliances.

Wind Power: Harnessing Africa's Winds for a Sustainable Future

In addition to solar energy, wind power is another renewable energy source with immense potential for Africa. The continent's long coastline and vast open plains offer ideal conditions for wind energy production. Countries like **Egypt**, **South Africa**, **Kenya**, and **Morocco** are already investing in wind power projects, and more nations are beginning to explore the possibilities of wind energy.

Harnessing the Winds of the Red Sea: Egypt's Wind Power Success

Egypt is one of the leading African nations in the development of wind power, with the **Gebel El-Zeit Wind Farm** being one of the largest on the continent. Located along the Red Sea coast, the wind farm generates hundreds of megawatts of electricity and contributes significantly to Egypt's renewable energy goals. The Egyptian government has set ambitious targets to increase its renewable energy capacity, and wind power is expected to play a central role in achieving these targets.

South Africa's Wind Energy Revolution

South Africa is another country where wind power is making significant strides. The country's **Renewable Energy Independent Power Producer Procurement Program (REIPPPP)** has attracted both local and international investors to develop large-scale wind farms. The **Jeffreys Bay Wind Farm**, for example, is one of the country's largest and is part of South Africa's broader efforts to reduce its dependence on coal and transition to cleaner energy sources.

South Africa's wind energy sector has also contributed to job creation, with many people employed in the construction, operation, and maintenance of wind farms. As the cost of wind energy continues to decline, it is expected that wind power will become an increasingly important part of the country's energy mix.

Solar and Wind Power: A Perfect Synergy

One of the key advantages of solar and wind energy is that they complement each other. Solar power is most effective during the day when the sun is shining, while wind power is often strongest at night or in the early morning hours. This complementary nature allows countries to maximize their renewable energy output by combining solar and wind farms.

In countries like **Kenya**, **South Africa**, and **Morocco**, where both solar and wind resources are abundant, combining these two sources of energy can provide a reliable and consistent supply of electricity. This integrated approach can help reduce reliance on fossil fuels and increase the stability of national grids.

Challenges and Opportunities for Scaling Up Renewable Energy

While the potential for solar and wind energy in Africa is enormous, there are several challenges that need to be addressed in order to fully realize this potential. These challenges include:

1. **Infrastructure:** Many African countries still lack the necessary infrastructure to support large-scale renewable energy projects, such as grid connections, transmission lines, and storage systems.
2. **Financing:** Renewable energy projects require significant upfront investment, and access to financing remains a barrier for many African nations. International partnerships and private-sector involvement are crucial for overcoming this challenge.
3. **Policy and Regulatory Frameworks:** Strong government policies and regulatory frameworks are essential to incentivize renewable energy development and attract investment.

Countries that have established clear renewable energy targets and favorable policies have seen more success in attracting investment.

4. **Skills Development:** There is a need for skilled workers to build, operate, and maintain renewable energy infrastructure. Investment in education and training programs is necessary to develop a local workforce capable of supporting the renewable energy industry.

The Future of Renewable Energy in Africa

Despite these challenges, the future of renewable energy in Africa looks bright. With abundant solar and wind resources, coupled with the increasing affordability of renewable energy technologies, Africa has the opportunity to leapfrog traditional fossil fuel-based energy systems and build a sustainable energy future.

Through investment in renewable energy, Africa can reduce its dependence on fossil fuels, improve energy access for millions, and contribute to global efforts to combat climate change. Solar winds are not just a metaphor—they are a vision for a cleaner, brighter, and more sustainable future for Africa and the world.

CHAPTER NINE

THE BIOTECH FRONTIER

Africa, often considered the cradle of humanity, is now poised to lead in a revolutionary field—biotechnology. With its vast biodiversity and rich natural resources, the continent is uniquely positioned to address health challenges that have long plagued its populations. From tackling diseases such as malaria, HIV/AIDS, and tuberculosis to advancing agricultural innovations for food security, Africa's biotechnology sector is expanding rapidly. This chapter explores the breakthroughs in biotechnology that are directly addressing the continent's health challenges, offering hope and sustainable solutions for millions of people.

Africa's Health Landscape: A Complex Challenge

Africa is home to some of the world's most pressing health challenges. Despite progress in healthcare, the continent still faces widespread diseases and limited access to quality medical care. Malaria, HIV/AIDS, tuberculosis, and neglected tropical diseases (NTDs) continue to ravage populations. Additionally, the prevalence of diseases like sickle cell anemia, which disproportionately affects people of African descent, requires innovative approaches to healthcare delivery and treatment.

In the face of these challenges, Africa has embraced biotechnology as a means to revolutionize its healthcare systems. The potential of biotechnology is vast: it can create new medicines, vaccines, diagnostic tools, and therapeutic interventions that are tailored to the unique needs of African populations.

Harnessing Africa's Biodiversity for Health Solutions

Africa's natural environment is a treasure trove of untapped resources that could offer solutions to many of the continent's health problems. The vast array of indigenous plants, animals, and microorganisms found across the continent holds enormous potential for the development of new medicines and treatments.

Traditional Medicine Meets Biotechnology

For centuries, African communities have relied on traditional medicine, using native plants and herbs to treat various ailments. In recent years, there has been a concerted effort to combine traditional knowledge with modern biotechnology to create more effective and sustainable health solutions. Research institutions across Africa are working to validate the medicinal properties of these plants through scientific studies, with promising results.

One notable example is the **African traditional herb Artemisia annua**, which has been used for centuries to treat malaria. Today, this plant is being researched as a potential source of a new generation of antimalarial drugs, which are critical in the fight against malaria. In countries like **Uganda** and **Tanzania**, partnerships between traditional healers and modern scientists are creating a new wave of research that integrates ancient wisdom with cutting-edge biotechnological methods.

Plant-based Drugs for Africa's Health Needs

Plants such as **Moringa**, **Baobab**, and **Neem** are increasingly being studied for their potential to treat conditions ranging from malnutrition to diabetes. In regions where healthcare infrastructure is limited, these plants may serve as accessible and affordable alternatives to expensive pharmaceutical drugs. Companies are emerging that specialize in the research, cultivation, and commercialization of plant-based treatments, helping local economies while addressing significant health needs.

Innovative Approaches to Malaria Control

Malaria continues to be one of the deadliest diseases in Africa, killing hundreds of thousands annually. In recent years, biotechnology has played a central role in developing new tools to combat the disease, focusing on prevention, diagnosis, and treatment.

Genetically Modified Mosquitoes

One of the most groundbreaking biotech solutions to malaria is the development of genetically modified (GM) mosquitoes. These mosquitoes are designed to either resist malaria transmission or reduce the population of mosquitoes carrying the malaria parasite. Projects like the **GeneDrive** initiative, which aims to alter the genes of mosquitoes to reduce malaria transmission, have gained international attention. Trials in countries such as **Kenya** and **Mozambique** are providing hope that malaria transmission can be significantly reduced in the coming decades.

Malaria Vaccines

Another major breakthrough in biotechnology is the development of the **RTS,S/AS01 malaria vaccine**, which has shown promise in clinical trials. This vaccine, developed in collaboration with the **World Health Organization (WHO)**, aims to reduce the burden of malaria in young children—especially in sub-Saharan Africa. Ongoing studies and increased funding for malaria vaccine development are bringing the world closer to a viable solution.

Addressing HIV/AIDS with Biotechnology

HIV/AIDS has had a profound impact on Africa, where over two-thirds of the global population living with the virus resides. Biotechnology has played a critical role in the ongoing battle against the disease, with innovations that have improved both treatment and prevention.

Gene Editing for HIV Cure

Advancements in gene editing technologies, such as **CRISPR-Cas9**, are now being explored as a potential cure for HIV/AIDS. Researchers in Africa are actively working on gene-editing strategies that could eliminate the virus from the body by targeting its genetic code. Trials are still in early stages, but the potential for a cure has sparked excitement within the African medical and scientific communities.

Prevention and Treatment: The Role of Biotechnology

In addition to gene editing, biotechnology has also revolutionized HIV prevention and treatment through the development of antiretroviral drugs (ARVs). These drugs are now more widely available across the continent, and the African market for ARVs is growing. Innovations in biotechnology have enabled the production of affordable generic versions of these life-saving drugs, making HIV treatment more accessible to millions of people living with the virus.

Furthermore, biotechnology is enhancing prevention strategies, including pre-exposure prophylaxis (PrEP) and post-exposure prophylaxis (PEP), both of which have become critical tools in the fight against HIV transmission. In addition to medication, biotechnology-driven diagnostic tests allow for quicker and more accurate detection of HIV, enabling earlier treatment.

Sickle Cell Anemia: Genetic Research and Treatment

Sickle cell anemia is another disease that disproportionately affects people of African descent. Biotechnology has made significant strides in understanding the genetic causes of sickle cell disease and developing potential treatments.

Gene Therapy for Sickle Cell

In recent years, advances in gene therapy have shown great promise in the treatment of sickle cell anemia. **CRISPR-Cas9** gene-editing technology, for instance, has been used in clinical trials to correct the genetic mutation responsible for sickle cell disease. If these trials prove successful, gene therapy could provide a permanent cure for millions of people suffering from this inherited blood disorder.

Stem Cell Research

Stem cell research is also providing new hope for sickle cell patients. In some African countries, stem cell transplantation is being explored as a treatment for sickle cell anemia, with promising outcomes. While these treatments are still in their infancy, they represent an exciting frontier for biotechnology in the field of genetic disorders.

The Future of Biotechnology in Africa

The breakthroughs in biotechnology that are emerging in Africa are not only addressing the continent's most pressing health challenges but also contributing to the global knowledge pool. As Africa continues to invest in research and development, it has the potential to become a global leader in biotechnology, particularly in areas like drug discovery, genetic research, and sustainable agriculture.

Africa's biotechnology frontier holds immense promise, and as the continent continues to push boundaries, it will undoubtedly redefine the future of global health. With continued investment and collaboration, Africa can turn its unique health challenges into opportunities for innovation, creating a healthier and more sustainable future for generations to come.

CHAPTER TEN
CULTURAL RENAISSANCE

In a world where globalization often leads to the erosion of indigenous cultures, Africa stands at the crossroads of preserving its rich heritage while embracing modernity. The digital age offers unprecedented opportunities to revitalize and showcase the continent's cultural wealth. This chapter explores the cultural renaissance in Africa, driven by technology and the innovative use of digital platforms. From music and dance to visual arts and storytelling, African artists and creators are redefining what it means to be African in the 21st century, balancing the preservation of traditions with the demands of modernity.

Africa's Cultural Heritage: A Tapestry of Richness

Africa's cultural heritage is vast and diverse, shaped by centuries of history, traditions, languages, and customs. From the ancient wisdom of the Egyptians to the drum rhythms of West Africa, the continent is home to a wealth of art forms, rituals, and oral traditions. However, with the rise of modernity and the influence of Western culture, there has been a growing concern about the erosion of these traditions.

For many years, African art and culture were underrepresented on the global stage. Local practices were often dismissed as "primitive" or "backward," and the influence of colonialism led to the devaluation of indigenous cultural expressions. Today, however, Africa is experiencing a cultural renaissance, fueled by the increasing recognition of the value of its artistic and cultural output. Technology, particularly digital platforms, plays a pivotal role in this revival.

Digital Platforms: The New Canvas for African Art

The internet and digital technologies have transformed the way African artists, musicians, filmmakers, and writers connect with audiences. Social media platforms, streaming services, and digital art platforms provide African creatives with a global stage to showcase their work. The power of technology allows artists to preserve, transform, and reinterpret traditional art forms, ensuring their survival for future generations.

Social Media as a Cultural Bridge

Platforms like **Instagram**, **YouTube**, and **TikTok** have revolutionized the way African artists share their work with the world. Musicians, dancers, and visual artists are now able to bypass traditional gatekeepers and reach audiences globally. The viral nature of these platforms allows African cultural expressions—whether through music videos, traditional dance challenges, or storytelling—to gain traction and visibility, uniting audiences from diverse backgrounds.

One notable example is the rise of **Afrobeats** music, which has taken the world by storm in recent years. Artists like **Wizkid**, **Burna Boy**, and **Tiwa Savage** have used digital platforms to reach millions of listeners globally, while also retaining strong connections to their African roots. The popularity of Afrobeats is a testament to the power of digital technology in promoting African culture and influencing global music trends.

Digital Archives: Preserving African Heritage

As much as technology helps preserve African culture, it also plays a crucial role in safeguarding intangible cultural heritage. Digital archives, online museums, and virtual galleries have become essential tools for documenting and preserving traditional African arts, languages, and rituals that are at risk of being lost. For example, **The Africa Digital Heritage Project** aims to digitize and preserve African art and cultural artifacts for future generations, providing global access to African cultural heritage.

Furthermore, universities, cultural institutions, and independent researchers are leveraging technology to document oral histories, traditional music, folklore, and indigenous languages that were once passed down orally. This digital archive serves as a valuable resource for future generations of Africans, ensuring that cultural knowledge is preserved and accessible worldwide.

Cultural Reclamation through Fashion and Design

African fashion has become one of the most visible expressions of the continent's cultural revival. Designers are combining traditional textiles and techniques with contemporary styles, creating a fusion of old and new that resonates globally. Digital platforms like **Instagram** and **Pinterest** have enabled African designers to showcase their collections to a global audience, challenging Western-centric notions of beauty and fashion.

For example, the use of traditional **kente** cloth from West Africa, **shweshwe** fabric from South Africa, and **ankara** prints have been reinterpreted in modern ways by young African designers. These designers are also using technology to collaborate, creating online fashion shows, virtual pop-up shops, and e-commerce platforms that bring African fashion to the international stage.

Additionally, African artisans and craftsmen are using digital tools to market their handmade goods—such as beadwork, pottery, and textiles—on platforms like **Etsy** and **Jumia**, reaching customers far beyond local markets. This digital transformation of traditional crafts is not only preserving cultural practices but also creating economic opportunities for artisans and communities.

Reclaiming African Storytelling in the Digital Age

Storytelling is at the heart of African culture, and the advent of digital platforms has allowed African storytellers to amplify their voices. African literature, folklore, and oral traditions are being reimagined and retold through novels, podcasts, film, and digital comics.

The rise of **African cinema**, with films such as **"Black Panther"** and **"Queen of Katwe"**, has showcased African narratives on a global scale. Streaming services like **Netflix**, **Amazon Prime**, and **YouTube** have made it possible for African filmmakers to reach global audiences, providing a platform for stories that challenge stereotypes and provide a more authentic representation of the continent.

Moreover, **podcasts** have become a popular medium for African storytellers to connect with listeners. Topics range from history and culture to social justice and contemporary issues, all narrated through the lens of African perspectives. Digital platforms also provide opportunities for African authors to publish e-books and audiobooks, expanding access to African literature worldwide.

The Role of Virtual Reality and Augmented Reality in Cultural Preservation

Virtual reality (VR) and augmented reality (AR) technologies are emerging as powerful tools for preserving and experiencing African heritage. VR allows users to virtually visit historical sites, museums, and cultural festivals, even if they are physically located on the other side of the world. AR, on the other hand, is being used to enhance the experience of African art and artifacts, creating immersive exhibitions that allow visitors to interact with cultural objects in new and engaging ways.

For example, the **Ghana Museum of African Art** uses VR technology to allow virtual tours of its collection, providing an interactive experience that brings African history to life. Similarly, **AR apps** are being developed to enhance cultural festivals and ceremonies, giving participants a richer, more immersive experience that connects them with African traditions and heritage in innovative ways.

A Future of Cultural Hybridization and Global Connection

As Africa embraces the digital age, the continent is experiencing a cultural hybridization—where traditional practices coexist and evolve alongside modern technological innovations. This hybridization is not just about the preservation of culture, but also about its evolution, adapting to global trends while retaining its authenticity.

The digital age is creating opportunities for Africa's culture to shine globally, allowing for cross-cultural collaborations, innovations, and exchanges that celebrate diversity while honoring tradition. African artists, musicians, filmmakers, and writers are reclaiming their narrative and redefining what it means to be African in a globalized world.

CHAPTER ELEVEN

THE EDUCATION REVOLUTION

Africa is on the cusp of an educational revolution, fueled by technology, innovation, and a growing recognition of the continent's potential. The traditional model of education, often shaped by colonial legacies and rigid systems, is evolving into a more inclusive and flexible approach that aims to democratize access to knowledge and learning. This chapter delves into the innovative learning models and technological advancements that are transforming African education, empowering students, and enabling them to participate in the global knowledge economy.

The Challenges of Traditional Education Systems in Africa

For many years, Africa's education systems have struggled with issues such as overcrowded classrooms, under-resourced schools, and a lack of access to quality learning materials. These challenges have contributed to high dropout rates, particularly in rural areas, and have left many young people without the skills needed to thrive in the modern world. The legacy of colonial education systems, which often prioritized rote learning over critical thinking and creativity, has further hindered progress in fostering a generation of thinkers, innovators, and problem-solvers.

However, as the digital age progresses, a new wave of educational reform is sweeping across the continent. Innovations in technology, new teaching methodologies, and a focus on inclusivity are providing Africa with the opportunity to reshape its education systems, making education more accessible, equitable, and relevant to the needs of the 21st century.

Technology as a Catalyst for Change

One of the most significant drivers of the education revolution in Africa is the rise of technology. Mobile phones, internet access, and digital learning platforms are helping bridge the gap in access to quality education. While many rural areas still face challenges in accessing traditional schools, mobile phones and online platforms are providing new opportunities for learning.

E-Learning and Online Courses

In many African countries, e-learning platforms are becoming a viable alternative to traditional classrooms. Platforms such as **Moodle**, **Coursera**, and **edX** offer students the opportunity to take courses from universities around the world, opening doors to knowledge that were once inaccessible. In countries like Kenya, Nigeria, and South Africa, e-learning is rapidly gaining traction, with both private and public institutions offering online courses that cater to diverse fields such as technology, business, and medicine.

A notable example is **Andela**, a technology company based in Africa that trains software developers through an online platform, connecting them with international companies seeking skilled workers. Through such platforms, African students are not only receiving valuable education but also gaining skills that are in high demand in the global job market.

Mobile Learning: The Power of the Cellphone

Africa has one of the highest mobile phone penetration rates in the world, with millions of people using smartphones and basic mobile devices. Leveraging this widespread use, mobile learning is becoming a powerful tool for educational transformation. Mobile-based learning applications are allowing students to access lessons, take quizzes, and even receive certifications, all from the palm of their hands.

In countries like Tanzania and Rwanda, mobile technology is being used to teach literacy, numeracy, and vocational skills to people in remote areas. Programs like **m-learning** (mobile learning) are helping to bridge the digital divide, offering personalized learning experiences for students at all levels, from primary school to university.

Innovative Learning Models: Beyond the Classroom

While digital platforms and technology are important, the education revolution in Africa is also characterized by innovative learning models that extend beyond the traditional classroom setting. These new models are designed to address the unique needs of African students, providing flexible, adaptive, and inclusive learning environments.

The Rise of Hybrid Learning

Hybrid learning, which combines in-person and online learning, is becoming increasingly popular in African education. This model allows students to access lessons both inside the classroom and remotely, making learning more flexible and adaptable to students' schedules. For example, many universities in Africa are offering hybrid courses, where students can attend lectures in person or watch them online, depending on their preferences and availability.

Hybrid learning is also enabling more students to attend school while balancing other responsibilities, such as work or family obligations. This flexibility is particularly important for women, who may face greater challenges in accessing education due to societal expectations and gender roles.

Project-Based Learning (PBL) and Experiential Education

Another innovative model gaining traction in Africa is **project-based learning (PBL)**. PBL emphasizes hands-on, practical learning, where students work on real-world projects that address local issues. This method encourages critical thinking, creativity, and problem-solving, skills that are essential for the workforce of tomorrow.

In many African countries, PBL is being integrated into school curricula to help students engage with the challenges facing their communities. For instance, students in Ghana and Uganda have worked on projects related to sustainable agriculture, clean energy, and water conservation, developing solutions to pressing environmental and social issues. This approach not only enhances students' learning experiences but also equips them with the skills and knowledge needed to contribute meaningfully to their communities.

The Role of Artificial Intelligence in Education

Artificial intelligence (AI) is beginning to play a transformative role in African education by providing personalized learning experiences and automating administrative tasks. AI-powered platforms are being used to assess students' learning styles, track their progress, and offer tailored content that suits their individual needs. For example, **Khan Academy** and **Duolingo** use AI to adapt lessons based on students' performance, ensuring that each learner receives the support they need.

In addition, AI is helping to improve teacher effectiveness. By automating grading and administrative tasks, AI allows teachers to spend more time on direct instruction and individualized support. AI-powered tools are also helping to identify students who are struggling and provide early interventions to help them succeed.

Bringing Education to the Margins

The digital revolution in African education is not just about creating new opportunities for those in urban areas; it is also about reaching marginalized communities, such as those in rural regions or in refugee camps. Mobile-based learning platforms and satellite internet are extending educational access to the farthest corners of the continent, allowing students who were previously excluded from the traditional education system to access quality learning materials.

Initiatives such as **BRCK** in Kenya and **Zoe in Ethiopia** are working to provide internet access in remote areas, ensuring that students in villages and underserved communities can participate in the educational revolution. In addition, NGOs and government agencies are working to provide laptops, solar-powered devices, and internet connectivity to students who would otherwise lack access to technology.

The Future of Education in Africa: A Global Perspective

The education revolution in Africa is just beginning, but it holds the potential to transform the continent in profound ways. As African students gain access to cutting-edge technologies and innovative learning models, they will be better equipped to navigate the challenges of the global economy.

At the heart of this revolution is the idea that education should not be a privilege, but a right. Technology, innovation, and inclusivity are the key drivers of this movement, and the future of African education is one where every student, regardless of their background, has the opportunity to reach their full potential.

CHAPTER TWELVE

URBAN UTOPIAS

In the evolving landscape of Africa's future, the concept of **smart cities** is emerging as a beacon of hope for sustainable development, technological innovation, and social progress. These urban utopias seek to harmoniously blend advanced technology with sustainable living practices, creating environments that are not only efficient but also equitable, resilient, and future-proof.

The Vision of Smart Cities

At the heart of Africa's urban utopias is the idea of **smart cities**—innovative urban spaces that use digital technology to improve quality of life, optimize resources, and enhance the sustainability of urban environments. Smart cities integrate **data-driven technologies**, **green energy solutions**, and **intelligent infrastructure systems** to address the pressing challenges of urbanization, climate change, and resource depletion.

With Africa's rapid population growth and urbanization, the demand for more efficient, livable cities is increasing. Today, over 40% of Africa's population lives in urban areas, and that figure is expected to rise significantly in the coming decades. Traditional city models are struggling to keep pace with this growth, leading to overcrowding, inadequate infrastructure, and limited access to essential services.

Smart cities, however, are designed to not only accommodate this growth but also provide better living conditions by integrating technology with sustainable urban planning.

Sustainable Infrastructure: Building the Foundations of Tomorrow

In these urban utopias, the focus is on creating **green infrastructure** that minimizes environmental impact while maximizing social benefits. Cities such as **Eko Atlantic City** in Nigeria and **Konza Techno City** in Kenya are leading the charge by incorporating sustainable building materials, energy-efficient buildings, and innovative transportation systems into their designs.

The integration of **solar energy, rainwater harvesting systems**, and **green roofs** in new city developments helps reduce the carbon footprint while providing sustainable resources for residents. These cities are also designed to be **energy-neutral**, with the aim of producing as much energy as they consume through renewable sources such as solar, wind, and hydroelectric power.

By embracing principles of **circular economy**, where waste is minimized and resources are reused, these cities aim to create closed-loop systems that are sustainable for generations to come.

Smart Technology: Enhancing Efficiency and Connectivity

Smart cities are, by definition, highly connected and data-driven environments. The integration of **Internet of Things (IoT)** devices, **artificial intelligence (AI)**, and **big data** analytics is transforming the way cities are managed, making them more efficient, responsive, and adaptive to residents' needs.

In urban utopias, data flows seamlessly to create smarter urban systems, enabling real-time monitoring of traffic patterns, energy consumption, waste management, and even public health. For example, **smart traffic lights** that adjust in real time to traffic flow, **automated waste collection** systems that optimize routes based on real-time data, and **smart meters** that monitor and control energy use are some of the innovations improving daily life.

One of the most exciting prospects of these technologies is the creation of **smart homes**, where everything from lighting to security to energy consumption can be controlled remotely via mobile apps. These homes are designed to be energy-efficient, integrating sustainable materials and intelligent systems to optimize resources and reduce waste.

Sustainable Mobility: Redefining Transportation in African Cities

Transportation is one of the most critical challenges facing African cities. Congestion, pollution, and inadequate public transport systems are common issues that detract from the quality of life for millions. Urban utopias address these issues by designing integrated, sustainable transportation networks that make use of the latest technologies.

Electric vehicles (EVs) and **e-bikes** are becoming increasingly common in smart city designs, offering environmentally friendly alternatives to traditional gasoline-powered vehicles. Furthermore, **shared mobility platforms**, such as ride-sharing apps and **autonomous vehicles**, are playing a significant role in reducing the number of private cars on the road, easing congestion, and lowering carbon emissions.

The **smart city mobility infrastructure** also includes high-speed, reliable **public transit** systems, including **electric buses** and **light rail networks** that make it easier for residents to navigate cities without relying on private vehicles. **Bike-sharing programs**, pedestrian-friendly walkways, and **green urban spaces** for recreational activities are other key elements of sustainable mobility in urban utopias.

Inclusivity and Social Equity: Building Cities for All

One of the most profound aspects of Africa's urban utopias is their focus on **social equity**. Smart cities are designed to be inclusive, ensuring that all residents—regardless of their socioeconomic background—have access to the benefits of technological advancements and sustainable living practices.

In these cities, social equity is embedded in urban planning. **Affordable housing** is integrated into the smart city infrastructure, ensuring that lower-income populations can also enjoy the benefits of clean energy, efficient transport systems, and access to healthcare and education. **Universal access to internet connectivity** is another key feature, as the digital divide remains a significant challenge in many African nations.

By prioritizing inclusivity, urban utopias aim to create spaces that encourage **social cohesion** and reduce inequality. These cities will provide equal opportunities for education, healthcare, employment, and civic participation, enabling all citizens to contribute to and benefit from the growth of their cities.

Urban Agriculture and Food Security: Cultivating the Future

In the face of rapid urbanization and climate change, urban agriculture is becoming a vital component of sustainable cities. Urban farming initiatives are cropping up in cities across Africa, utilizing vacant lots, rooftops, and community gardens to produce local, fresh food.

Vertical farming, **hydroponics**, and **aquaponics** are technologies being used to grow food in urban environments, reducing the reliance on external food sources and increasing food security. These practices not only promote sustainability but also provide fresh, nutritious food to urban populations, cutting down on the carbon footprint of food transportation.

Urban agriculture also offers opportunities for **community engagement**, as local residents work together to cultivate crops and strengthen social bonds. In some African smart cities, urban farming is integrated into the design of residential neighborhoods, offering spaces for people to grow their own food while reducing environmental impact.

Challenges and Opportunities: Paving the Way Forward

While the vision of smart cities is promising, significant challenges remain. For one, the implementation of such ambitious projects requires substantial financial investment, collaboration between public and private sectors, and political will. Additionally, there are concerns around **data privacy**, **security**, and **surveillance** in highly connected cities, which must be addressed to ensure that the benefits of smart cities are felt by all.

However, these challenges also present opportunities for African nations to shape the cities of the future in ways that are uniquely suited to their cultures, environments, and social needs. The development of urban utopias can also create opportunities for innovation, job creation, and economic growth, positioning Africa as a leader in the global urban development movement.

The dream of urban utopias is not just a distant ideal but an achievable goal for Africa's future. With the right blend of technology, sustainability, and inclusivity, Africa's cities can evolve into vibrant, resilient urban spaces that serve as models for the rest of the world. As African nations continue to develop and innovate, these urban utopias will offer a glimpse of a future where technology and humanity coexist harmoniously, and cities become places where people can live, work, and thrive in a sustainable, inclusive environment.

CHAPTER THIRTEEN

THE ETHICAL ALGORITHM

As Africa embraces the digital revolution and positions itself as a leader in technological innovation, the development of **Artificial Intelligence (AI)** has become a focal point. However, with the rapid growth of AI comes a pressing challenge: ensuring that these systems reflect **African values, ethics**, and **cultural perspectives**. The question is not just about building advanced AI technologies but also about how to integrate ethical considerations into their design and deployment in ways that align with the continent's unique history, identity, and social realities.

The African Perspective on AI and Ethics

Artificial Intelligence, in its essence, seeks to mimic human intelligence and decision-making processes. But the frameworks that shape AI—its algorithms, data inputs, and decision-making rules—are often grounded in values that reflect the cultures and priorities of the societies that develop them. For much of the AI industry, this has traditionally meant Western values and perspectives.

In Africa, however, there is a growing recognition that **ethical AI** should not be a one-size-fits-all approach. The continent's diverse cultures, belief systems, and historical experiences must inform how AI systems are designed, programmed, and used. Thus, the question of what constitutes "ethical" AI becomes more complex and requires careful thought about the **social, economic**, and **cultural implications** of the technology.

African ethical principles, such as **Ubuntu**, which emphasizes community, interconnectedness, and shared humanity, could offer a unique lens through which AI can be shaped. Ubuntu highlights values like empathy, compassion, and respect for the dignity of others, which could serve as guiding principles for designing AI systems that prioritize social good and **human flourishing** over profits or technological advancement alone.

Building AI with African Values: A Framework for Ethical Algorithms

The creation of AI systems that embody African values requires a conscious effort to integrate **ethical principles** into every stage of AI development—starting from data collection and algorithm design to decision-making processes and deployment in real-world applications.

1. **Cultural Sensitivity**: One key component is ensuring that AI systems respect and reflect the diversity of Africa's cultures. This involves designing algorithms that can understand and engage with local languages, traditions, and social norms. A good example would be creating AI tools that respect local customs in healthcare, education, and commerce, rather than imposing standardized solutions that may not be culturally relevant.

2. **Transparency and Accountability**: In the context of AI, African societies may prioritize **transparency** and **accountability**—ensuring that decisions made by AI are traceable, explainable, and justifiable. African governments, businesses, and communities must have the power to **audit** and understand the decisions made by AI systems, ensuring that these systems are used fairly and without bias.

3. **Inclusivity and Accessibility**: A key element of ethical AI in Africa is ensuring **inclusive access**. As the continent continues to tackle issues of inequality, it is essential that AI does not reinforce existing social divides. Ethical AI should be designed to **empower marginalized communities**, particularly those who have historically been excluded from the benefits of technological advancement.

4. **Bias and Fairness**: One of the most significant concerns with

AI is the potential for **bias**—particularly in systems that rely on large datasets that may not accurately represent African contexts or populations. AI systems trained on biased data can perpetuate harmful stereotypes and inequalities. The development of **fair AI systems** must involve the careful curation of diverse datasets that reflect the **complex realities** of African life, ensuring that AI technologies are not discriminatory.

5. **Human-Centered AI**: African values often center around **human dignity**, and thus AI must be designed to enhance, rather than undermine, human capabilities. This is reflected in an emphasis on **collaboration** between humans and machines, where AI acts as a **tool** to assist and complement human efforts, rather than replace them entirely. This approach fosters the idea that technology should serve humanity, not the other way around.

AI in Africa: Opportunities and Ethical Dilemmas

As Africa makes strides in AI development, it faces several key opportunities and ethical dilemmas that must be carefully navigated.

Opportunities:

1. **Economic Growth**: AI can drive economic development by enabling greater productivity, creating jobs, and boosting innovation across sectors such as agriculture, healthcare, finance, and education. For example, AI-driven tools in **agriculture** can help farmers increase crop yields and reduce waste, while AI-powered health diagnostics can provide access to high-quality medical care in underserved regions.
2. **Social Development**: AI can be leveraged to improve access to education and social services, providing innovative solutions to long-standing challenges. By prioritizing African ethics, AI tools can be developed to support social enterprises,

NGOs, and governments in addressing issues like **poverty**, **healthcare**, and **food security**.
3. **Technological Leadership**: Africa has the opportunity to lead the global conversation on **ethical AI** by creating a **model** for AI development that prioritizes fairness, equity, and inclusivity. This leadership can help position Africa at the forefront of global technological progress and innovation.

Ethical Dilemmas:

1. **Data Privacy and Surveillance**: The use of AI raises important concerns about privacy, especially in countries where laws regarding **data protection** are still developing. The ability of AI systems to collect and analyze vast amounts of personal data presents risks in terms of **surveillance**, **identity theft**, and **exploitation**. African nations must work together to create robust frameworks for **data privacy** that balance the benefits of AI with the protection of individual rights.
2. **Job Displacement**: As AI technologies automate many tasks traditionally carried out by humans, concerns about **job displacement** are rising. The potential for **unemployment** in certain sectors may have a disproportionate impact on marginalized communities. Therefore, it is crucial to design policies that promote **AI-driven job creation** and provide **retraining opportunities** for workers affected by automation.
3. **Ethical Governance**: The question of who governs AI in Africa is critical. Ethical AI development cannot be left solely to private tech companies; it must involve **collaboration** with governments, **civil society**, and **local communities** to ensure that AI systems reflect diverse interests and not just corporate priorities. The governance of AI should be guided by African ethical frameworks, ensuring that AI benefits all citizens, particularly the **disenfranchised**.

Case Studies: AI in Action in Africa

Several African countries are already making strides in implementing AI technologies with an ethical focus. For example:

- **Kenya** has launched AI-powered mobile health services, which provide **affordable healthcare** in rural areas, tackling issues like **maternal health** and **disease diagnosis**. These solutions are designed to be accessible to **low-income populations** and are rooted in local healthcare needs.
- **South Africa** is using AI to address issues of **financial inclusion**, enabling more people to access **banking services** and credit through AI-powered systems that assess risk and financial behavior beyond traditional credit histories.
- **Nigeria** is exploring the ethical implications of AI in areas such as **law enforcement** and **criminal justice**, focusing on how to ensure that AI systems do not perpetuate existing biases in the justice system.

In the pursuit of AI-driven progress, Africa must ensure that ethical considerations are embedded in the development process from the ground up. The unique cultural, historical, and ethical landscapes of African societies provide a rich foundation for designing AI systems that are not only technologically advanced but also ethically sound.

The development of the **ethical algorithm** will require collaboration, careful deliberation, and a commitment to ensuring that AI serves the needs of the many, not just the few. By drawing on African traditions, values, and principles, AI can become a powerful force for good—helping to build a **future that is equitable**, **inclusive**, and **sustainable**.

CHAPTER FOURTEEN

THE HEALTH NEXUS

In the 21st century, the world faces numerous health challenges, many of which disproportionately affect **African nations**. From infectious diseases like **HIV/AIDS, malaria**, and **tuberculosis**, to the rising burden of non-communicable diseases like **diabetes, hypertension**, and **cancer**, the continent has long struggled to address healthcare issues. However, a new era of collaboration and innovation is emerging, where **technology, global partnerships**, and **African ingenuity** are converging to tackle these health crises and transform the healthcare landscape.

The concept of a **Health Nexus** refers to the dynamic intersections between **technology, policy, global partnerships**, and **local innovations** that are coalescing to provide solutions to Africa's health challenges. Through a combination of **telemedicine, artificial intelligence (AI), mobile health technologies**, and **collaborations with international organizations**, African nations are not only confronting health challenges but are also setting the stage for a **revolution in healthcare delivery** across the continent.

Africa's Health Challenges: A Complex Landscape

Africa's health challenges are multifaceted and interconnected. The continent's healthcare systems have long been hampered by limited access to medical services, shortages of healthcare professionals, inadequate infrastructure, and weak health policies. **Rural areas** are particularly vulnerable, with millions of people lacking access to even basic health services. Additionally, the rise of **global pandemics** like **COVID-19** has further exposed the fragile nature of healthcare systems across the continent.

However, while the challenges are significant, they also present opportunities for transformative change. The African **Health Nexus** represents a convergence of different forces—**technology, collaboration**, and **innovation**—working in tandem to overcome these obstacles and redefine healthcare delivery in Africa.

Technology-Driven Solutions for Health Crises

1. **Telemedicine and Remote Healthcare** One of the most significant technological innovations in Africa's healthcare landscape has been the rapid adoption of **telemedicine**. In regions with limited access to medical facilities or qualified healthcare professionals, **telemedicine** platforms enable patients to receive consultations via mobile phones, computers, or video calls. This technology has been particularly valuable during the **COVID-19 pandemic**, when lockdowns and social distancing measures made it difficult for people to visit healthcare facilities.

Telcoms and **mobile health apps** have bridged the gap in providing access to primary care, mental health services, maternal health consultations, and even **specialist care** through digital platforms. **Kenya's M-TIBA**, for example, allows people to store and transfer money for health services, ensuring that **healthcare financing** is accessible to all, especially those in **low-income communities**.

1. **Artificial Intelligence (AI) and Data Analytics AI** has become a game-changer in the fight against health crises in Africa. From **predictive analytics** that identify outbreaks of diseases like **malaria** and **Ebola** to AI-driven diagnostic tools that assist doctors in diagnosing diseases faster and more accurately, **AI** is revolutionizing the healthcare space. In countries like **South Africa**, AI is being used to **predict patient outcomes,** improve medical imaging, and analyze large datasets to detect patterns that might otherwise go

unnoticed.

Moreover, **data analytics** can help **predict disease outbreaks** and track vaccination efforts, making it possible for governments and health organizations to respond more swiftly and efficiently. By leveraging both **big data** and **machine learning**, African nations are taking steps to improve the **efficiency**, **accuracy**, and **reach** of their health systems.

1. **Mobile Health (mHealth) Solutions Mobile health (mHealth)** technologies, which harness the power of **smartphones** and **mobile networks**, are playing a critical role in improving healthcare access in Africa. With the rapid expansion of **mobile phone penetration** across the continent, many countries are leveraging mHealth apps to provide **health education**, **tracking tools**, and **treatment reminders** to millions of users.

One prominent example is **mTrac**, a mobile application used in **Uganda** to monitor **health supplies**, track **disease outbreaks**, and collect **health data** from remote areas. Similarly, **mobile applications for HIV management**, such as **Infectious Disease Tracker (IDT)** in **Kenya**, help patients track their medications and appointments, while providing healthcare workers with up-to-date information on treatment adherence.

Global Partnerships for Health Innovation
While Africa has seen considerable progress in healthcare through technological innovation, it is clear that **collaboration with global partners** is essential for scaling these innovations across the continent. Global health organizations, governments, NGOs, and private sector

players are increasingly recognizing the importance of **collaborating with African countries** to address health challenges.

1. **The Global Fund**: The **Global Fund to Fight AIDS, Tuberculosis, and Malaria** has played a pivotal role in supporting African countries in their fight against infectious diseases. Through funding, partnerships, and technical assistance, the Global Fund has helped to scale **health interventions**, including **diagnostics**, **treatment**, and **prevention** strategies across the continent. This partnership has been particularly instrumental in combating **HIV/AIDS** and **malaria**.
2. **Bill & Melinda Gates Foundation**: The **Gates Foundation** has invested heavily in **healthcare innovation** in Africa, with a focus on **vaccination, maternal health**, and **child health**. One example is the foundation's **support for the development of new vaccines** for diseases such as **malaria** and **diarrheal diseases**, which disproportionately affect African children. By partnering with local governments, universities, and healthcare organizations, these efforts are helping to build sustainable health systems across the continent.
3. **World Health Organization (WHO)**: The WHO has been instrumental in supporting African nations with technical guidance, resources, and coordination during health crises like **Ebola outbreaks** and the **COVID-19 pandemic**. By providing **training** and **capacity building** for local healthcare workers, the WHO has helped to improve the **quality of care** and ensure that countries are better prepared for future health challenges.
4. **Pharmaceutical Companies**: In the fight against **diseases**, global pharmaceutical companies are increasingly partnering

with African governments and research institutions to develop and distribute **affordable medications**. For example, the partnership between **Johnson & Johnson** and various African governments has led to innovative solutions for tackling diseases such as **HIV** and **tuberculosis**.

The Future of the Health Nexus: Sustainability and Local Innovation

As African countries continue to partner with global organizations and leverage technological advancements, the future of healthcare in Africa looks promising. However, it is important that this future is not just shaped by external forces but by local **innovations** and **sustainability**.

1. **Homegrown Solutions**: While global partnerships are crucial, African nations must also focus on developing **homegrown solutions** that address the specific health challenges of the continent. Local innovations, such as **affordable diagnostic tools, biotechnology solutions**, and **telemedicine services**, are already making a significant impact in places like **Nigeria, Ghana**, and **Ethiopia**. Governments should invest in **local research** and **entrepreneurship** to foster a self-sufficient healthcare ecosystem.
2. **Sustainability**: The success of the Health Nexus will depend on the **sustainability** of these partnerships and technological solutions. This includes ensuring that **local healthcare workers** are trained and equipped to use the new technologies, that infrastructure is built to support them, and that **health systems** are strengthened to provide **ongoing care** and support.
3. **Community Engagement**: The success of technological innovations in healthcare will depend on **community buy-**

in and **participation**. Communities must be engaged in the design and implementation of health solutions to ensure that they are culturally appropriate and widely accepted. Local leaders, healthcare workers, and patients themselves must be part of the conversation to ensure that solutions are both effective and relevant.

The **Health Nexus** is a powerful model for transforming healthcare in Africa, combining **technology**, **innovation**, and **global partnerships** to tackle the continent's most pressing health challenges. As Africa continues to embrace this new era of healthcare delivery, it is critical that these solutions are designed to be sustainable, inclusive, and responsive to the unique needs of the continent's people.

By embracing technology and fostering collaborations, African nations are not only addressing immediate health crises but also **building resilient health systems** that can adapt to future challenges. As we move forward, the lessons learned from the Health Nexus will serve as a beacon for other regions of the world, showing how **global collaboration** and **local innovation** can come together to create a healthier future for all.

CHAPTER FIFTEEN

THE SPACE ODYSSEY

Africa's journey into space exploration is a bold and exciting chapter in the continent's ongoing narrative of innovation, resilience, and global collaboration. For much of the 20th century, space exploration was dominated by the space agencies of Europe, the United States, Russia, and China. However, as the 21st century unfolds, Africa is steadily positioning itself as a player in the global space race. The continent is beginning to embrace the transformative potential of space technologies—not only for national pride but also for advancing its development in critical sectors like **telecommunications, agriculture, health, education,** and **climate monitoring.**

Africa's ventures into space are not just a vision for the future; they represent the **convergence of ambition, technological investment**, and the strategic realization that space exploration can become a powerful tool for **socio-economic progress**. In this chapter, we explore Africa's burgeoning space program, the **scientific breakthroughs** already taking place, and how the continent is harnessing the wonders of space to improve life on Earth. Africa is not merely a passive observer of the space age; it is becoming an active participant, with significant strides being made across the continent in space exploration, satellite technology, and international cooperation.

Africa's Space Pioneers: A New Dawn for the Continent

1. **The African Space Program: A Unified Vision:** The African Space Program, coordinated by the **African Union's African Space Policy and Strategy**, is a collective initiative to harness the continent's natural resources and human potential for

space exploration. The vision of **"Africa in Space"** is one that embraces not just space exploration, but also the broader application of space science and technology to enhance life on Earth.

In **2017**, the African Union established the **African Space Agency (ASA)** to consolidate efforts and focus on promoting space-related activities across member states. With its headquarters in **Addis Ababa, Ethiopia**, the ASA serves as the continent's primary institution for advancing space research, coordinating satellite launches, and developing space infrastructure that can benefit multiple sectors of African society.

1. **Key Milestones in Africa's Space Journey**
    - **Nigeria** made history in 2003 with the launch of **Nigerian Communications Satellite-1 (NIGCOMSAT-1)**, becoming the first African nation to independently launch a communication satellite. This event marked the beginning of Africa's entry into space, setting a precedent for future satellite launches.
    - **South Africa** has long been a leader in space research, with its **South African National Space Agency (SANSA)** playing a significant role in **space weather monitoring, satellite development**, and **space science research**. In 2018, South Africa launched its **SumbandilaSat**, a high-resolution Earth observation satellite, which helped monitor **climate change**, **agriculture**, and **natural resource management** across the continent.
    - **Kenya** launched its first satellite, **1KUNS-PF**, in

2018. This small satellite was developed with the help of the **University of Nairobi** and the **Japan Aerospace Exploration Agency (JAXA)**. The launch symbolizes Kenya's growing space capability and marks a significant achievement for East Africa in the global space arena.
2. **The Rise of Space Technologies and Innovations** Space technologies are often seen as tools of **geopolitical power** and **technological prestige**, but for Africa, they are transforming lives in more practical ways. The application of space science is far-reaching, touching numerous sectors of African life.

Satellite Technology plays a key role in improving **communications** in rural and remote areas. **Telecommunications satellites** ensure that people living in even the most isolated communities can access **internet**, **radio**, and **television**, bridging the digital divide. Moreover, **satellite imagery** has become a vital tool for monitoring **agriculture, disaster management, natural resources**, and even **climate change** patterns.

Space-based solutions for climate monitoring have been instrumental in helping African governments track and mitigate the effects of **extreme weather** events, such as **droughts, floods**, and **storms**. The data provided by **Earth observation satellites** is vital for improving agricultural practices, ensuring food security, and managing **water resources** across the continent.

1. **Leveraging Space Science for Sustainable Development** Africa's engagement with space exploration is closely linked to the **United Nations' Sustainable Development Goals (SDGs)**. The application of space science and technology

holds great potential for advancing these goals, especially in areas such as:

- **SDG 2: Zero Hunger**: Satellites help monitor **crop health**, **soil moisture**, and **weather patterns**, enabling farmers to make more informed decisions about planting and harvesting, and ultimately improving food security across Africa.
- **SDG 13: Climate Action**: Space technology provides accurate, up-to-date data on climate conditions, helping African nations adapt to and mitigate the effects of **climate change**. For example, **satellite-based early warning systems** can help predict droughts and floods, allowing communities to better prepare and reduce losses.
- **SDG 9: Industry, Innovation, and Infrastructure**: By investing in space technologies, African countries are enhancing their **technological infrastructure** and creating new industries in satellite development, space tourism, and other space-related sectors, contributing to economic growth and job creation.

2. **Space Exploration as a Pathway to Innovation and Economic Growth** The potential economic benefits of space exploration are immense. The space sector is a significant driver of **technological innovation**, creating opportunities for the **private sector**, **research institutions**, and **entrepreneurs** to develop new products, services, and industries. With the rise of **space tourism, mining resources from asteroids**, and the growing demand for satellite services, space exploration can become an economic engine for the continent.

African governments are beginning to recognize that **space technology** is not just a matter of prestige, but a tool for **economic diversification** and **long-term growth**. The establishment of space-related **industries**, including **satellite manufacturing**, **space tourism**, and **rocket launching facilities**, is creating new opportunities for skilled jobs in **STEM (science, technology, engineering, and mathematics)** fields across Africa.

1. **Collaboration and International Partnerships** Africa's entry into space is not happening in isolation. The continent is forming **partnerships** with space-faring nations and institutions around the world. Collaborations with organizations such as the **European Space Agency (ESA)**, **NASA**, and **the Russian space agency (Roscosmos)** are providing the technical expertise and resources needed to help African countries develop their space programs.

Additionally, partnerships with **private companies** in the **global space sector**, such as **SpaceX**, **Blue Origin**, and **Arianespace**, are opening up new avenues for satellite launches and technology transfers, enabling African nations to build their own **space infrastructure** without having to rely solely on external assistance.

1. **The Role of Education and Innovation Hubs** Africa's burgeoning space industry has sparked a wave of interest in **space science education** across the continent. Universities and research institutions are increasing their focus on **aerospace engineering**, **astronomy**, and **astrophysics**, with the goal of producing a new generation of African space scientists and engineers.

Innovation hubs in cities like **Cape Town, Lagos**, and **Nairobi** are emerging as centers for **space tech startups**, where young African entrepreneurs are developing innovative space-related technologies and applications. These hubs are fostering a culture of **innovation** and **collaboration**, creating opportunities for **cross-border partnerships** and building an ecosystem of **space professionals** across the continent.

The Future of Africa's Space Odyssey

Looking ahead, Africa's space exploration efforts will continue to evolve, driven by the **need for technological advancement, collaboration**, and **sustainable development**. As the continent makes further strides into space, it will face challenges, including the **need for infrastructure, funding**, and **capacity building**. However, with **strong political will, international partnerships**, and **homegrown innovations**, Africa is well-positioned to become a key player in the space race of the future.

The **Space Odyssey** is not just about reaching the stars—it is about harnessing the power of space to improve life on Earth, create economic opportunities, and contribute to solving the world's most pressing challenges. Africa's space journey has only just begun, and the possibilities are as limitless as the cosmos itself.

CHAPTER SIXTEEN

THE DIGITAL DIVIDE

The promise of a **digitally connected Africa** is one of the most exciting prospects for the continent's future. Technology has the potential to transform economies, empower communities, and democratize access to information and opportunities. Yet, despite rapid advancements in digital infrastructure, a significant **digital divide** persists across the continent. This divide highlights the disparities in access to **technology**, **internet connectivity**, **digital literacy**, and **innovation opportunities** between different regions, socio-economic groups, and generations.

In this chapter, we explore the causes and consequences of the **digital divide** in Africa, examining the **economic**, **social**, and **political factors** that have shaped its current state. We also highlight the innovative solutions being implemented to bridge this gap, ensuring that all African populations, regardless of their background, can participate in the digital revolution.

The Scope of the Digital Divide in Africa

1. **Geographical Disparities** The digital divide in Africa is often shaped by **geographical factors**. Urban areas are typically well-served by digital infrastructure, with **high-speed internet, mobile networks**, and **advanced tech hubs** flourishing in cities like **Nairobi, Lagos, Cape Town**, and **Accra**. However, rural areas continue to face significant challenges when it comes to accessing the same level of **connectivity, affordable devices**, and **digital services**. The **rural-urban divide** is one of the most profound aspects of the digital gap, leaving millions of Africans in remote areas with limited access to life-changing technologies.

2. **Economic Barriers Affordability** remains a key issue in

overcoming the digital divide. The cost of **smartphones**, **computers**, and **data plans** is often prohibitively high for many people in Africa, especially in lower-income households. In some cases, the price of a **smartphone** or **internet subscription** can represent a substantial portion of an individual's income, making technology out of reach for the majority of the population. Furthermore, limited access to **electricity** in certain areas further compounds the problem, as it is difficult for people to charge devices or access the internet without a reliable power supply.

3. **Education and Digital Literacy** Another critical aspect of the digital divide is the lack of **digital literacy** among large segments of the African population. While some African countries have made significant strides in integrating **technology into education**, many schools and communities still lack access to the training necessary to use digital tools effectively. **Digital skills** are increasingly becoming a prerequisite for **employment, economic mobility**, and participation in the digital economy. However, the gap in **digital literacy** creates unequal opportunities for African youth and adults, further entrenching the disparities between the technologically connected and disconnected segments of society.

4. **Gender and the Digital Divide** Gender disparities in access to technology is another facet of the digital divide in Africa. **Women and girls** in certain regions, particularly in **rural** and **conservative** areas, often face cultural and economic barriers that limit their access to digital tools and education. These barriers range from **limited exposure** to technology in early childhood to **gendered expectations** around the use of smartphones and computers. As a result, many women are unable to fully participate in the digital economy or benefit

from the educational and social opportunities that technology can provide. This **gender gap** in technology access not only stifles the potential of women but also hinders broader societal progress.

The Impact of the Digital Divide

1. **Economic Exclusion** The digital divide has far-reaching implications for economic inclusion and development. **Limited access** to technology and **internet connectivity** means that many individuals and communities are excluded from participating in the **digital economy.** E-commerce, **online banking**, and **digital entrepreneurship** offer incredible opportunities for economic growth, yet those without access to these platforms are often left behind. This gap exacerbates existing inequalities and reinforces cycles of poverty.

For small businesses, the lack of access to **digital tools** and **online marketing platforms** hinders their growth and competitiveness, particularly in a globalized world where digital presence is often a key driver of success. Farmers, artisans, and other small-scale entrepreneurs who cannot access **e-commerce platforms** or **digital financial services** are left at a disadvantage in the modern economy.

1. **Educational Barriers** The **digital divide** also significantly limits access to quality **education**. As **online learning** becomes increasingly common, particularly in the wake of the COVID-19 pandemic, those without reliable internet access are often unable to participate in educational opportunities. In rural areas, schools may not have the resources to incorporate **digital tools** or provide remote learning options.

Without access to technology, students are not only deprived of educational content but also of the **skills** necessary to thrive in the digital world.

This **lack of access to education** creates a cycle of **inequality**, as young people in underserved communities miss out on opportunities for self-improvement, employment, and economic advancement.

1. **Social and Political Implications Exclusion from digital platforms** also has social and political consequences. Access to information, news, and public discourse is increasingly moving online. Without reliable internet access, large segments of the population are unable to engage with important political discussions, access government services, or participate in the **democratic process**. The digital divide, therefore, exacerbates the **information gap**, leaving disadvantaged groups at the mercy of traditional, often less accessible, sources of information.

Solutions to Bridging the Digital Divide

Despite the challenges, many innovative solutions are emerging across Africa to bridge the digital divide. Governments, **NGOs**, **private companies**, and **community leaders** are implementing initiatives aimed at ensuring equitable access to technology and digital opportunities for all Africans, especially those in underserved areas.

1. **Affordable Internet Access** Several African countries are focusing on making **internet access** more affordable and widespread. Programs like **Google's Project Loon** (which provides **internet access through high-altitude balloons**) and **Facebook's Internet.org** are working to extend connectivity to remote and rural areas. Additionally,

government initiatives, such as **universal broadband plans** and **subsidized data packages**, are beginning to lower the cost of internet services for low-income communities.

Public-private partnerships are crucial in improving internet infrastructure in rural areas, where connectivity is still limited. Mobile network operators, in collaboration with **government** and **private companies**, are expanding networks and building more **mobile towers** in underserved regions.

1. **Digital Literacy Programs** In response to the digital skills gap, a growing number of **digital literacy programs** are being implemented across Africa. These initiatives focus on providing **technology education** to youth, women, and marginalized communities, ensuring they can access and benefit from the digital world. Programs such as **Coding for Africa, Tech Hubs**, and **African Digital Skills Programs** are empowering young Africans with the skills needed to excel in **STEM fields** and participate in the digital economy.

In addition, **universities** and **technical schools** are increasingly offering specialized programs in **software development, data science, artificial intelligence**, and other digital fields, providing young Africans with the tools they need to succeed in a technology-driven world.

1. **Gender-Sensitive Approaches** To address the gender gap in technology access, a number of initiatives are specifically targeting women and girls. **STEM scholarships, women-led tech hubs**, and **female entrepreneurship programs** are helping to empower women and ensure they have equal access to the digital tools that will shape their futures. Additionally,

gender-inclusive digital literacy programs are encouraging young girls to explore careers in **technology**, ensuring that Africa's digital revolution is equitable and inclusive.
2. **Community-Driven Solutions** Many solutions to the digital divide are emerging from local communities. **Community networks** and **mobile learning hubs** are being set up to provide internet access, digital tools, and **training** in underserved areas. Local leaders are organizing **grassroots initiatives** that focus on making technology accessible to all, even in the most remote parts of the continent.

The Road Ahead

Bridging Africa's digital divide is not just about providing access to technology—it's about creating a truly **inclusive digital ecosystem** that empowers everyone to benefit from the opportunities the digital world offers. While progress is being made, much work remains to be done. The future of Africa's digital transformation depends on continued investment in **affordable infrastructure**, **education**, **policy frameworks**, and **collaborations** that ensure no one is left behind.

As Africa moves forward, the digital divide must no longer be seen as an insurmountable challenge, but as an opportunity for innovation, collaboration, and growth. The digital future of Africa is within reach, and with concerted efforts from all sectors of society, it is one that can be shared equitably across the continent.

CHAPTER SEVENTEEN

THE INNOVATORS' GUILD

In a future Africa marked by technological renaissance, the **Innovators' Guild** stands as the epicenter of creative brilliance, entrepreneurial ingenuity, and visionary leadership. This chapter delves deep into the stories of African inventors, entrepreneurs, and changemakers who are driving the continent's technological surge, transforming industries, communities, and economies. These individuals are not merely shaping Africa's future—they are reimagining it, breaking the molds of conventional thinking, and redefining the narrative of technological advancement in Africa.

Africa's innovation ecosystem has historically been undervalued, often overshadowed by stereotypical depictions of poverty, instability, and technological lag. However, in the wake of new opportunities and digital transformation, a **new generation of African innovators** has emerged. From **startups** in **Silicon Savannahs** to high-tech laboratories in **Cape Town** and **Lagos**, African inventors and entrepreneurs are leading the charge in **artificial intelligence, biotechnology, renewable energy, agritech, e-commerce,** and **fintech.**

Breaking the Molds: Pioneering African Innovators

1. **The Spirit of Innovation in Africa** Innovation in Africa isn't born out of a vacuum. It arises from a deep well of **ingenuity, resourcefulness**, and the desire to **solve local problems** with locally sourced solutions. For centuries, Africans have demonstrated the ability to adapt to their environment, invent tools, and develop systems that make life more sustainable. This same spirit is now evident in the growing innovation hubs across the continent, where ideas are transforming into world-changing solutions.

These innovators are building solutions that bridge the gap between **traditional knowledge** and **modern technologies**, using indigenous wisdom to enhance technological applications. The innovation is rooted in **practicality**—designed to address issues like **healthcare access, food security, affordable energy, education**, and **climate change**, while also fostering economic growth and job creation.

1. **Profiles of the Game-Changers**
    - **Dr. Thomas B. C. D. Kipruto** (Kenya)
    A leading **biotech inventor**, Dr. Kipruto developed a groundbreaking **biomedical sensor** that monitors **blood sugar levels** in diabetic patients without the need for needles. His invention has revolutionized the **healthcare sector** in Africa, especially in rural areas where access to medical facilities is limited. His work has led to affordable, non-invasive medical devices that are saving lives and making healthcare more accessible to millions.
    - **Juliana Rotich** (Kenya)
    One of the co-founders of **BRCK**, a company that provides **internet access** to remote and underserved regions of Africa. Rotich has pioneered the development of **rugged, portable Wi-Fi routers** designed to operate in areas with unreliable electricity and limited internet connectivity. Through **BRCK**, she's making **internet access** more affordable, practical, and reliable for students, entrepreneurs, and communities that have been left out of the digital revolution.
    - **Iyinoluwa Aboyeji** (Nigeria)

A **serial entrepreneur** and one of the co-founders of **Andela**, a company that trains software developers in Africa and connects them with global tech firms. Aboyeji is at the forefront of Africa's **digital talent export industry**, playing a key role in creating a global **tech workforce** from Africa. His efforts have fostered the growth of **technology hubs** in cities like **Lagos** and **Nairobi**, providing opportunities for young Africans to become leaders in the digital economy.

- **Tayo Oviosu** (Nigeria)
  Founder of **Paga**, a mobile payments company that has transformed how Nigerians and other Africans send money, pay bills, and conduct financial transactions. Paga's mobile wallet system has made **financial services** accessible to millions who were previously excluded from the traditional banking system. Oviosu's innovation is empowering people across the continent to achieve **financial inclusion**, reducing poverty, and driving economic development.

2. **Empowering Women Innovators** Women innovators in Africa are playing a transformative role in driving technological growth. In a traditionally male-dominated field, **African women** are breaking barriers, challenging stereotypes, and leading projects that make an immense impact in sectors like **agriculture**, **healthcare**, and **education**. Despite facing significant obstacles like **gender inequality**, limited access to funding, and cultural constraints, women like **Fatimah Aliyu** (Nigeria), **Wendy Luhabe** (South Africa), and **Rita Nandhi** (Uganda) are shaping the future with bold ideas.

- **Fatimah Aliyu**, for example, is the founder of **GrainHub**, a platform designed to connect **smallholder farmers** with buyers, thus addressing food security challenges across **Northern Nigeria**. GrainHub leverages **mobile technology** to increase efficiency in the agriculture supply chain, empowering farmers and providing them with access to **market prices, financing**, and **logistical support**.
- **Wendy Luhabe** is an influential figure in South Africa's **social entrepreneurship** space. She has driven initiatives that use **technology** to address **socio-economic issues** related to **education** and **health**. Her work focuses on improving **sustainable business models** while helping women in rural areas access financial services and entrepreneurial opportunities.

3. **The Role of African Tech Hubs and Incubators** Africa's **technology hubs** and **incubators** have become critical ecosystems where innovators thrive. These hubs are nurturing the next generation of African tech entrepreneurs by providing them with the tools, resources, and mentorship needed to scale their ideas. From **Lagos** to **Nairobi, Cape Town** to **Accra**, these centers have become focal points for the growth of the **digital economy** in Africa.

- The **Meltwater Entrepreneurial School of Technology** (MEST) in **Accra, Ghana** offers training, **seed funding**, and **mentorship** to budding tech entrepreneurs across the continent. The school's alumni have gone on to build successful tech companies that are impacting sectors such as **agriculture, finance**, and **e-commerce**.

- The **iHub** in **Nairobi, Kenya**, is another example of a vibrant tech hub fostering digital innovation. It provides **co-working spaces, incubation programs**, and **access to funding** for early-stage startups. The iHub is home to some of Kenya's most successful tech entrepreneurs, including the creators of **M-Farm, M-KOPA Solar**, and **Twiga Foods**.

4. **Innovators in Emerging Fields:** the African innovation landscape is also seeing significant strides in **emerging technologies** like **blockchain, artificial intelligence**, and **renewable energy**. Innovators are not only addressing Africa's challenges but also pioneering solutions that have global relevance.
    - **Blockchain and Fintech Innovations**
    Mthuli Ncube, the Finance Minister of Zimbabwe, advocates for the use of **blockchain technology** to provide **secure, transparent financial systems** that combat corruption and promote financial inclusion. **Chinonso Eze**, co-founder of **Blockchain Academy Africa**, is spearheading **blockchain education** and **training** for African professionals, positioning the continent as a key player in this emerging field.
    - **AI for African Solutions**
    Kagiso Kweyama is using **artificial intelligence** to drive healthcare solutions in South Africa, applying AI-powered algorithms to **predict disease outbreaks**, improve **patient outcomes**, and enhance **medical research**.

Building an Ecosystem of Innovation

The **Innovators' Guild** is more than just a collection of individuals; it is an ecosystem of collaboration. **Governments, universities,**

venture capitalists, and **global tech companies** are all playing a crucial role in nurturing Africa's burgeoning innovation landscape. By fostering an environment that values **creativity, collaboration**, and **inclusivity**, Africa is on track to become a global leader in innovation.

To accelerate this growth, there is a need for more **investment** in **tech education, innovation hubs**, and **support systems** that enable African innovators to **scale** their ideas and bring them to market. This includes improving **access to capital, partnerships with global tech giants**, and creating **policies** that support innovation across all sectors.

The Road Ahead

As Africa continues to rise as a global innovation hub, it is clear that the future belongs to the **innovators**. These game-changers are not only **leading the digital revolution** within Africa—they are **transforming the global technological landscape**. With continued investment in **education, infrastructure**, and **entrepreneurship**, Africa's **Innovators' Guild** will have a profound and lasting impact on the world.

CHAPTER EIGHTEEN

THE CYBER FRONTIER

In the rapidly advancing digital age, where technology increasingly shapes every aspect of life, Africa's rise as a global tech leader comes with a pressing challenge: **cybersecurity**. As the continent pushes forward in the realms of **digital innovation, e-commerce, artificial intelligence**, and **renewable energy**, protecting its digital infrastructure has become as crucial as the technologies themselves. This chapter delves into the complex and dynamic field of **cybersecurity**, exploring the measures that African nations are taking to safeguard their technological assets, protect personal data, and defend against emerging digital threats.

Africa's Digital Transformation: A Double-Edged Sword

Africa's **cybersecurity landscape** is shaped by the paradox of rapid technological adoption and the lag in developing robust protective measures. On one hand, the continent is experiencing a **digital renaissance**, with increasing access to the internet, mobile devices, and cloud computing, driving economic growth and enhancing lives. On the other hand, this rapid adoption presents a **vulnerable frontier**—one that must be carefully guarded against threats like **data breaches, hacking, identity theft**, and **cyber-attacks**.

As Africa's tech ecosystems grow, so do the risks. With greater connectivity comes greater exposure to malicious actors, both within and outside the continent, looking to exploit weak points in digital infrastructure. For instance, **ransomware attacks, phishing schemes**, and **online fraud** are becoming more common as Africa's reliance on digital platforms intensifies.

Building Cybersecurity Capacity in Africa

1. **National Cybersecurity Strategies**

The foundation of Africa's cybersecurity efforts lies in national **cybersecurity strategies** that set the tone for the protection of digital assets. These strategies are designed to establish **legal frameworks, institutions**, and **policies** that guide and protect the continent's growing digital economy.

- **Kenya**, for example, established the **Kenya Cyber Security Strategy** in 2014, which has since led to the creation of the **Kenya Cyber Security Centre** (KCSC). The KCSC plays a critical role in monitoring and addressing cyber threats, as well as providing guidance on how to protect national infrastructure.
- Similarly, **Nigeria** has introduced the **National Cybersecurity Policy and Strategy**, which aims to address the growing number of cyber-related crimes and enhance the resilience of Nigeria's digital infrastructure.

These strategies go beyond simply defending against external threats—they also aim to build **resilience**, enhance **cyber hygiene**, and foster a culture of **responsible digital usage**.

1. **The Role of Governments in Strengthening Cybersecurity**

Government involvement in cybersecurity in Africa is crucial, as it creates an enabling environment for innovation while ensuring safety and trust in digital systems. African governments are working on a **multilateral** approach to cybersecurity, collaborating with international bodies, regional organizations like the **African Union (AU)**, and private sector players to protect critical infrastructure, prevent cybercrime, and create laws that promote the **ethical use of technology.**

- The **African Union Convention on Cyber Security and Personal Data Protection**, which was adopted in 2014, provides a comprehensive framework for member countries to implement cybersecurity policies and strengthen the protection of personal data. It seeks to **harmonize** cybersecurity practices across the continent and promote cooperation among African nations in combatting cyber threats.

1. **Cybersecurity Education and Awareness**

One of the key components of building a resilient digital ecosystem is **education**. Africa faces a significant **skills gap** in the field of cybersecurity, as the demand for skilled professionals far exceeds the supply. Addressing this gap requires focused efforts to educate and train individuals in the **technical and policy aspects** of cybersecurity.

- **African universities** and **training institutions** are increasingly offering specialized degrees and certifications in **cybersecurity**, aimed at equipping the next generation of experts who can defend against cyber threats. Programs like **TechWomen Africa** in Kenya, **Cyber Security Centre of Excellence** in Nigeria, and **South Africa's Cybersecurity Academy** are working to **equip students** with the skills needed to tackle cyber threats head-on.
- Additionally, governments and organizations are investing in **cybersecurity awareness campaigns** that aim to educate the general public on safe digital practices, protecting personal data, and avoiding cybercrimes.

1. **The Role of the Private Sector in Cybersecurity**

The private sector in Africa plays an equally vital role in fortifying digital infrastructure. Companies in sectors such as **banking, telecommunications, energy,** and **e-commerce** are increasingly prioritizing cybersecurity. The rapid adoption of **cloud computing, mobile payment systems,** and **online banking** necessitates advanced protection measures to avoid financial losses, breaches of privacy, and damage to reputations.

- **Fintech companies** like **Flutterwave** and **Paystack** are leading by example in establishing advanced cybersecurity systems that protect users' financial data and ensure compliance with global standards.
- **Telecom giants** like **MTN** and **Vodacom** are also stepping up their efforts, investing in secure networks, adopting **encryption technologies,** and regularly conducting vulnerability assessments to protect their customers and systems from cyber-attacks.

1. **Emerging Threats and Innovations in Cybersecurity**

As technology evolves, so too do the threats. **Artificial intelligence (AI), machine learning,** and **Internet of Things (IoT)** are reshaping both the attack and defense landscape in the realm of cybersecurity. With the increasing deployment of **smart devices, connected homes,** and **autonomous systems,** the potential for new vulnerabilities grows.

- For instance, **AI-powered attacks** can automate and scale threats, making them harder to detect and prevent. On the defensive side, **AI and machine learning** can be harnessed

to detect abnormal activities, predict potential attacks, and respond in real time.
- In response to these evolving challenges, African cybersecurity experts are exploring the use of **blockchain** for secure data transactions, **quantum encryption** for unbreakable communication channels, and **biometric identification** systems to authenticate digital identities.

1. **Cybercrime and Cybersecurity Law Enforcement**

Cybercrime is a growing concern across the continent, and **cyber law enforcement** is key to tackling this issue. Many African nations are strengthening their legal frameworks to address issues such as **identity theft, cyberbullying, online fraud**, and **digital espionage**.

- **Interpol** and national **cybersecurity agencies** are increasingly collaborating to track down cybercriminals who operate across borders, using a **combination of legal cooperation** and advanced **forensic technologies**.
- Countries like **South Africa** and **Ghana** have introduced **cybercrime laws** to regulate online activities and hold offenders accountable. However, there is still work to be done to standardize cybercrime laws across the continent and ensure they remain relevant in the face of constantly changing technology.

Towards a Secure Digital Future
As Africa becomes a global leader in technology, it must also **prioritize cybersecurity** to secure its digital future. The **Cyber Frontier** is not only about **defending digital assets** but also about creating an environment of trust that fosters further innovation,

investment, and development. Governments, the private sector, and individuals must work together to create a **cyber-resilient Africa**, one where technology can flourish safely, securely, and ethically.

CHAPTER NINETEEN
THE GLOBAL STAGE

As Africa continues to harness the power of technology and innovation, its role on the **global stage** evolves from one of under appreciation to one of leadership and influence. The narrative of Africa's future is no longer one of dependency, but rather one of **empowerment** and **partnership**. This chapter delves into how Africa's growing **technological prowess** is reshaping its influence on international policy, economics, and diplomacy, marking the continent's shift from the periphery to the **center** of global discussions.

Redefining Africa's Global Identity

For centuries, Africa's image on the world stage has been shaped by **colonial legacies, political instability**, and **economic challenges**. However, the dawn of the 21st century brings a new era of opportunity, driven by the continent's technological revolution. With nations like **Nigeria, Kenya, South Africa**, and **Egypt** leading in **digital infrastructure, innovation**, and **entrepreneurship**, Africa is beginning to carve out a new identity on the world stage.

This transformation is driven not just by economic growth, but by the continent's ability to leverage **technological advancements** to **redefine global power dynamics**. As African nations adopt cutting-edge technologies and **drive digital economies**, they are positioned to become powerful **players in international policy, trade negotiations**, and **global economic governance**.

Africa as a Hub of Technological Innovation

Africa is no longer a **consumer** of technology—it is now a **producer**. The continent's rapidly growing **tech hubs**, such as **Silicon Savannah** in Kenya, **Yabacon Valley** in Nigeria, and **Cape Town's Tech District**, are evidence of Africa's burgeoning status as a leader in innovation. These hubs have given rise to an entrepreneurial spirit that transcends borders, connecting African innovators with global investors, partners, and markets.

Startups in industries ranging from **fintech** and **agritech** to **healthtech** and **edtech** are gaining international recognition for their **unique solutions** to Africa's specific challenges, and their ability to scale globally. African companies are increasingly **exporting technology solutions**, disrupting traditional markets, and redefining industries.

This trend of African nations becoming exporters of technology creates an opportunity for **soft power**—through technology and knowledge sharing, Africa can engage with other regions in ways that challenge the traditional narrative of dependency.

Africa's Role in Global Economic Policy

As the world faces a host of global challenges, including **climate change**, **economic inequality**, **health crises**, and **geopolitical instability**, Africa's growing technological capacity places the continent in a strong position to influence international economic policy.

1. Digital Trade and E-Commerce

Africa's increasing **digital trade** offers the continent new leverage in global trade discussions. The **African Continental Free Trade Area (AfCFTA)**, which aims to create a single market across the continent, can harness digital technologies to **simplify trade processes**, **reduce tariffs**, and **promote cross-border commerce**.

By creating seamless **digital payment systems** and **e-commerce platforms**, African countries can streamline trade, making it easier for local businesses to participate in the global economy. This will not only foster growth in **small- and medium-sized enterprises (SMEs)** but also **increase Africa's influence** in global markets.

1. Africa's Role in the Global Supply Chain

As the world shifts towards **digital economies**, Africa's role in the global supply chain is being transformed. The **continent's abundant natural resources**, coupled with a growing workforce skilled in digital technologies, positions Africa as a strategic partner in the global production of **electronics**, **renewable energy** systems, and **advanced manufacturing**.

By creating **smart manufacturing systems** and investing in **robotics, artificial intelligence (AI)**, and **IoT**, African nations can modernize their industries and increase their capacity to participate in high-value sectors of the global supply chain. This is also contributing to the emergence of new sectors such as **smart farming** and **blockchain-based trade systems**.

1. A Seat at the Global Economic Table

The rise of Africa as a global **economic power** is solidified through initiatives such as the **G20** and **BRICS**, where African nations now have a larger voice. South Africa's participation in **BRICS** and the **African Union's collaboration with China** through the **Belt and Road Initiative (BRI)** underscores the continent's growing diplomatic presence.

Africa's technological growth provides new avenues for **economic collaboration**, allowing African nations to strengthen their partnerships with **emerging economies** like **China, India,** and **Brazil**, while also forming new alliances with traditional global players in **Europe** and the **United States**. This interconnectedness creates a platform for Africa to shape global economic policies that reflect the continent's **aspirations** and **priorities.**

Africa's Voice in Global Climate Policy

Climate change is one of the most pressing challenges facing the world today. Africa, despite being the least responsible for global emissions, is disproportionately affected by the impacts of climate change, including **droughts**, **floods**, and **food insecurity**. However, Africa's growing technological innovation offers a unique opportunity to **drive global solutions** for climate change mitigation and adaptation.

1. **Renewable Energy Leadership**

African nations are increasingly turning to **renewable energy sources**, such as **solar, wind,** and **hydropower,** to power their economies and reduce dependence on fossil fuels. By investing in **clean energy technologies**, African countries are positioning themselves as leaders in the global fight against climate change.

- **Kenya** and **Morocco** are already leading the way in **solar energy** projects, while **South Africa** has established itself as a regional hub for **wind energy.**

1. **Tech-Driven Climate Solutions**

The continent's growing expertise in **environmental technologies**—such as **sustainable agriculture**, **water purification**, and **eco-friendly construction materials**—is contributing to a **global climate agenda** that prioritizes sustainability. Through **digital platforms** and **big data analytics**, African innovators are developing **smart solutions** to help tackle climate challenges while creating economic opportunities.

Global Diplomacy: Leveraging Technology for Soft Power

Africa's technological rise offers the continent a new form of **soft power**. Through **digital diplomacy**, African countries can influence global policy and shape the international narrative. By building **international partnerships** based on mutual respect, **knowledge sharing**, and **collaboration**, Africa can promote its **developmental agenda**, forge new economic relationships, and advocate for solutions to global challenges.

1. Cultural Diplomacy and Innovation

African nations are using **culture**, **technology**, and **innovation** to promote their national brands and attract foreign investment. The rise of **African cinema**, **music**, and **fashion**, combined with cutting-edge **digital media platforms**, is helping shift the global perception of Africa as a cultural powerhouse. Countries like **Nigeria** and **South Africa** are using the **digital arts** as a tool for international diplomacy, showcasing the continent's creativity while establishing strong ties with global audiences.

Shaping the Future: Africa as a Global Leader

Africa's growing **technological influence** is no longer a distant dream—it is becoming a reality. By continuing to innovate, collaborate, and leverage its **technological capacities**, Africa is poised to become a powerful player on the **global stage**, influencing international policy, economics, and global discourse. As African nations continue to embrace technology, the continent will not only secure its future but also shape the future of the world.

CHAPTER TWENTY

A NEW DAWN

As we approach the final chapter of this narrative, it is essential to pause and reflect on the journey we've undertaken—a journey of **transformation**, **resilience**, and **vision**. Africa, once seen as a land of untapped potential, is now poised to lead the world in the realms of **technology**, **innovation**, and **sustainability**. This chapter is a celebration of the continent's remarkable **rise**, as well as a hopeful look toward the future, a future where Africa's technological renaissance creates **boundless opportunities** for its people and for the world.

The Journey of Transformation

The story of Africa's transformation is not a story of sudden change, but one that has been shaped by **decades** of **struggles**, **dreams**, and **dedication**. It is a story of young minds pushing the boundaries of what was once thought impossible, of communities coming together to tackle **systemic challenges**, and of governments, businesses, and individuals embracing new ways of thinking. From the **Silicon Savannahs** of Kenya to the **renewable energy revolutions** in North Africa, the seeds of change have been planted and are now beginning to bloom into vibrant, thriving ecosystems of **innovation** and **growth**.

In the previous chapters, we have explored the ways in which Africa has embraced **technology** to address its unique challenges—**digital entrepreneurship**, **sustainable agriculture**, **renewable energy**, and **space exploration**, among others. But perhaps most importantly, we have seen how Africa has been able to integrate its rich **cultural heritage** and **ancient wisdom** with **cutting-edge innovations**, creating a harmonious blend that is uniquely African yet universally relevant.

This **transformation** is not just about technology—it is about a deeper, more fundamental change in the way Africa perceives itself and is perceived by the world. As **African entrepreneurs** lead the way in **fintech, healthcare, education,** and **green technologies,** the continent is being redefined. The once-bleak narrative of **poverty, conflict,** and **dependence** is being replaced with a story of **empowerment, partnership,** and **possibility.**

Limitless Possibilities Ahead

The future for Africa is indeed bright, but it is not merely bright because of technological advancements. It is bright because Africa's transformation is rooted in the **potential of its people**—youthful, vibrant populations eager to lead, innovates, and make a difference. Africa's burgeoning **tech hubs** are a testament to the **incredible creativity, entrepreneurial spirit,** and **resilience** that define the continent's young generation.

As we stand at the threshold of this new era, Africa's **limitless possibilities** are already unfolding. With **strategic investments** in **digital infrastructure, education,** and **innovation,** the continent will continue to build the **human capital** necessary for sustainable development and global competitiveness. The **African Union, private sector,** and **international partners** are all working together to ensure that Africa not only **leads in technology** but also benefits from it in ways that foster **inclusive growth, economic independence,** and **social equity.**

Africa's role as a **global player** in the **technological revolution** is not just a possibility—it is a certainty. As African nations **redefine global norms,** they will shape the future of **artificial intelligence, quantum computing, renewable energy, digital trade,** and **global diplomacy.** Africa's **influence** in international **policy** and **economics** will continue to expand, making it a powerful force for good in the world.

Unity in Diversity: The African Model

One of Africa's most significant strengths lies in its **diversity**—not only of cultures, languages, and traditions but also in its ability to **unite** and **collaborate**. This model of **unity in diversity** is a core principle that underpins Africa's **technological revolution**. Across the continent, people from different backgrounds are coming together to build a **shared future**, transcending historical divisions and working toward common goals.

This unity—whether through the **African Continental Free Trade Area (AfCFTA)** or the growing presence of **pan-African tech companies**—is creating a strong foundation upon which Africa can build its future. It is also an example to the world that **collaboration**, **inclusive development**, and **respect for diversity** can produce outcomes far greater than the sum of individual efforts.

A Call to Action: Building the Future Together

The new dawn for Africa is not only the responsibility of its leaders, its entrepreneurs, or its innovators—it is a responsibility that falls on all of us, as individuals and as a collective. This is a call to **action**, to actively participate in the creation of a future where **technology** serves the needs of the many, not just the few. Whether through **policy-making**, **education**, **research**, or **community development**, everyone has a role to play in shaping the Africa of tomorrow.

As the world becomes more interconnected, **Africa's voice** will be heard in **global councils**, **economic summits**, and **climate discussions**. Africa will not just be a **recipient** of aid, but a **leader** in **global solutions**. The continent's **technological prowess** will not only change the lives of Africans but will also contribute to solving some of the world's most pressing issues—from **climate change** to **healthcare** to **digital access**.

Africa's rise on the **global stage** is not a fleeting moment—it is a **transformation** that will shape the world for generations to come.

Conclusion: The Endless Horizon

In the distance, the horizon stretches far, offering an endless array of possibilities. As Africa enters this new dawn, it stands poised to not only redefine itself but to **reshape the future** of humanity. This is the beginning of an era where **technology**, **culture**, and **sustainability** intersect, and where Africa leads the charge toward a more prosperous and **inclusive global future**.

The journey is just beginning, and the possibilities ahead are limitless. The dawn of tomorrow is not a distant dream—it is Africa's new reality.

And as the sun rises, it is Africa's time to shine.

Don't miss out!

Visit the website below and you can sign up to receive emails whenever Emmanuel Dumbuya publishes a new book. There's no charge and no obligation.

https://books2read.com/r/B-A-PUGFD-TIGUF

BOOKS 2 READ

Connecting independent readers to independent writers.

Did you love *Glimmers of Distant Stars*? Then you should read *Kylian Mbappé*[1] by Emmanuel Dumbuya!

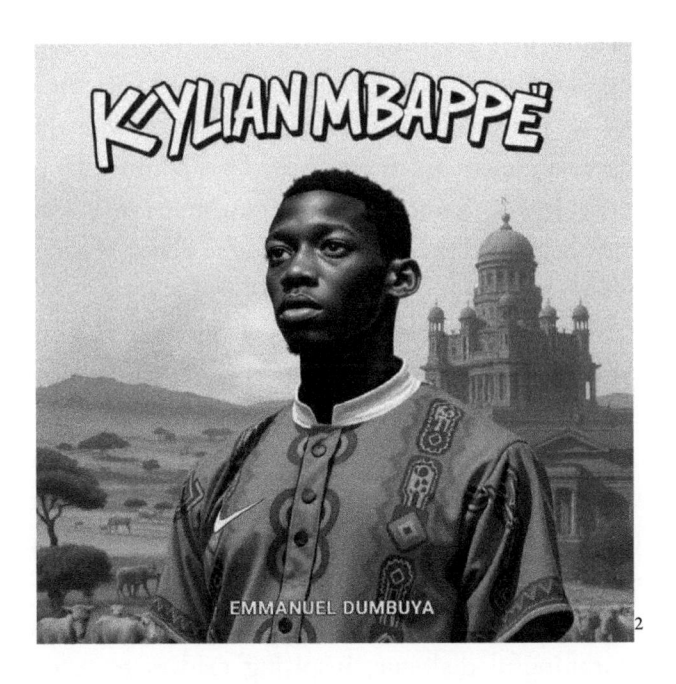

The journey of African history is one of profound resilience, transformation, and an unwavering spirit that has withstood centuries of hardship. In *Kylian Mbappé*, this narrative weaves together the intricacies of colonialism's enduring impact on Africa, its lingering scars, and the powerful legacy that continues to shape the identities of the continent's people. Through the eyes of Kylian Fofana, a young man whose dreams reach beyond borders while remaining deeply anchored in his cultural heritage, this novel encapsulates the struggles, triumphs, and moments of reconciliation that define the modern African experience.

---

1. https://books2read.com/u/31XzXW

2. https://books2read.com/u/31XzXW

At the heart of this story is the exploration of the complex relationship between colonized societies and their colonizers—a relationship that, despite its violent history, ultimately reveals the shared humanity that persists beneath the surface. Through Kylian's journey, the narrative invites readers to reflect on the profound intersections of personal and collective histories, where the bonds between past and present are never severed but continually evolve. It is a story that honors the richness of African culture, the unbreakable ties that span continents and the ongoing dialogue between generations, as old wounds seek healing and new possibilities are born.

Kylian Mbappé is not merely a tale of one man's journey; it is a tribute to the vibrant, multifaceted tapestry of Africa's past, present, and future. It speaks to the resilience of African peoples, their ability to rise from the ashes of oppression, and their relentless pursuit of a better tomorrow. Through Kylian's personal story, we are reminded that the echoes of history are never far behind, yet they are always accompanied by the hope of renewal.

May this novel serve as both a catalyst for deep reflection and a call for meaningful dialogue, inspiring readers to reconsider the interconnectedness of all human experiences. Let it remind us that while we cannot change the past, we hold the power to shape the future through our collective stories, our shared histories, and our enduring commitment to justice and unity.

Read more at https://www.amazon.com/-/e/B0DPR9HGHJ.

Also by Emmanuel Dumbuya

Africanah
Obelisk
Pandemic
The African Market
Kylian Mbappé
Glimmers of Distant Stars
Offline Souls: Escaping the Digital Noise

Watch for more at https://www.amazon.com/-/e/B0DPR9HGHJ.

About the Author

Emmanuel Dumbuya is a seasoned educator, author, and advocate with over a decade of experience in curriculum development and educational leadership. With a Master of Education in Curriculum Development and a focus on enhancing quality education in Sierra Leone, Emmanuel has dedicated much of his career to improving educational outcomes, especially for marginalized communities. His expertise spans curriculum design, instruction, policy analysis, and community engagement, and he has contributed significantly to educational reform efforts in Sierra Leone and beyond.

In addition to his work as an educator, Emmanuel is a passionate writer and has authored multiple textbooks on topics ranging from education to social justice.

His professional journey is credited to his radical approach, in exploring ways to integrate future skills into African curriculum frameworks, and mentoring youth as they prepare for the challenges of tomorrow's world.

Read more at https://www.amazon.com/-/e/B0DPR9HGHJ.

About the Publisher

An independent author passionate about storytelling, I am dedicated to creating narratives that inspire, educate, and ignite meaningful conversations. My works often explore themes of gender equality, empowerment, and social justice, particularly within the African context.

Through my writing, I aim to amplify voices that are often overlooked, weaving stories that celebrate resilience, challenge norms, and envision a more inclusive future. I believe in the power of words to transform perspectives and foster understanding across cultures and communities.

Whether you're exploring my fiction or nonfiction works, I hope you find stories that resonate with your experiences and inspire you to reflect on the world around you. Thank you for being part of this journey.

Email:emmanueldumbuya1@gmail.com / +23276453739
Read more at https://books2read.com/odumzbooks.